The Cost Of Love

A Common Man's *Love Story*

Saurabh Singh

Invincible Publishers

First published in India in 2017 by Invincible Publishers

ISBN: 978-93-86148-90-2

Invincible Publishers

G - 120, Sushant Lok III, Sector 57, Gurgaon-122002

Opposite Kasturba Ashram, Radaur Distt Yamuna Nagar, Haryana- 135133

Digitally Printed at Replika Press Pvt. Ltd.

Dedication

To the Brave Hearts of India

About the Author

* * *

Saurabh Singh is a Technical Marketing engineer by profession at a product company based in Hyderabad. He hails from the steel city of Jharkhand, Bokaro Steel City.

He is also the author of "College 2 Company... journey of an engineer". 'The Cost of Love' is his second fiction novel inspired by Nirbhaya case.

Get in touch with him through his website www.saurabhsinghonline.com or drop an email at saurabhdadon@gmail.com.

Acknowledgment

❄ ❄ ❄

This book is very close to my heart. Having said that, there are people who have always encouraged me to live my dreams and have always supported me throughout in this journey.

First and foremost, my wonderful parents, for tolerating my nuisances. And my in-Laws, for always encouraging me to pursue my dreams and guiding their daughter to do the same!

My beloved wife, Bhavna, for taking yet another challenge which decreased the amount of time I could spend with her. For being patient and giving me enough time and space to write this novel. And definitely, for playing the critics role so that I could improve upon my storyline.

To my beloved Bhaiya – Bhabhi- Aarav, Didi- Jiju- Aarush, for always being there whenever I needed them.

I thank God for pushing me into problems, testing me and finally pulling me out. *Heartiest Thanks to:* My friends-cum- editors, Prakhar, Ila, Lamha and Deepanshu, for helping me with the initial editing. Tejas, Ranjan, Manish Nagamani and Vivek for all their motivations.

Ramakrishna Tummanapelly, for an excellent cover

photography.

Dabloo, Dhiru, Sudhanshu, Sachin, and Abhishek for promising a word-of-mouth marketing. Markan, for just being there with me and supporting me in every possible way.

Thanks to my colleagues and friends for creating a wonderful and creative workplace.

Ajay, Bhavna and Sneha- The team of Invincible Publishers, for shaping my script in the best possible way and guiding me throughout the process. You guys rock!

And finally, thanks to all of you for picking up this book among others on the shelf!

Chapter-1

5-Days more

❄ ❄ ❄

"Do you want to say anything in your defence?" asked Justice Verma, while adjusting his glasses. Mediapersons and my parents, who were sitting in the front row, all looked at me for my response. I was really tired. My eyes turned red. Severe pain in my spine was not letting me stand straight. From the past seventeen days, I was given third degree at the Uttam Nagar Central jail in Delhi.

I held the barricade and looked at my parents. I could see their moist eyes and read the prayers on their shaking lips. Perhaps, they had a last hope that I would speak a word in my favour.

"No Sir," I said in a firm tone looking straight into the eyes of my mother.

A deep silence engulfed the courtroom. My mom was meek and quiet;

tears dropping down on her cheeks expressed her fear of losing me forever.

"Listening to all the verdicts and going through all the evidences, convict, Aaryan Rathod, is found guilty under IPC Sections 302 and 304.The convict is found guilty for brutal murder of Himanshu Joshi and rape of a 28-year-old-girl. Hence, this court sentences, Aaryan Rathod, death penalty. The convict to be hanged till death at early hours of December 24, 2013. This court is adjourned," said Justice Verma and broke the pen's nib. He stood and looked into my eyes. He was surprised to see the silence on my face.

My mom, on listening to the judgment, fainted. Nikhil, my best friend and colleague too, got hold of her and looked at me with teary eyes.

"May I see my mother once before you take me to the cell," I pleaded to the guards, who came to handcuff me. They looked at the jailor for permission.

"Let him go," said Jailor Shafaquat Ali. He was a tall, bearded and religious person. I used to call him Ali Sir. He was the only individual to whom I talked to in the jail. He always urged me to tell my side of story to the Judge. But, I simply ignored. Perhaps, I had decided to die.

"Ma, please. Don't cry. I can't see you crying," I said, sprinkling water over her face. She slowly came to her senses. She was shaking with fear of losing me. She grabbed my arms tightly and looked at me.

"I can't let you go. I can't see you dead," cried my mother, pressing her head to my chest. I hugged her tightly and cried my heart out.

"Have you ever thought how will I see your dead body? I brought you home when you were only 6 days old," mom said with a shaking voice.

She lifted her hands to show how she used to cradle

me in her arms.

"Now, they will hand me your dead body," said my mother and this time she broke down completely. I hugged her tightly in my arms and kissed her forehead.

"Forgive me this time Ma, I promise; in next life I will fulfill all your dreams," I said wiping her tears. My father, a retired government employee, and indeed a strong person, put his hand over my shoulder. I stood up to embrace him, the last time.

"Please take care of yourself and Ma. I am sorry Papa, I am sorry," I cried. He hugged me tightly and said, "I don't know if you are right or wrong. But,you will always be there in our hearts, and my son, for me you cannot be a criminal, you can never be." I could notice his wet eyes. This was the first time I saw him crying.

Nikhil stepped forward and hugged me. We didn't speak a single word for nearly two minutes. Perhaps, we both were living our last moments together.

"What will I say to Aarushi?" whispered Nikhil in a shaky voice. I stood still for a while and then took the pen from Nikhil's pocket.

"Ali Sir, can I have a piece of paper?" I asked. He picked a paper from the pile kept on a table and passed it to me.

"The day when you will know the truth, I may not be there with you, but my soul will always be around you; they will just hand over my body to you."

"Pass this on to Aarushi, if she asks for me. And tell her to forgive me for leaving her alone," I said, folding the paper and keeping it inside Nikhil's pocket. We gave each other a last hug.

"It's time to go," said Ali Sir, and gestured the guards to handcuff me. I wiped my tears and touched the feet of my parents for their last blessings. This time, they couldn't bless me, "*Jeete Raho*," (live long).

My parents and Nikhil hugged me until; I was forcibly pulled away from their arms.

I walked towards the cell, which was made for convicts sentenced to death, and slowly the sound of my mother's cry faded. These two minutes of my journey from the courtroom to the cell brought all the memories back.

"This is your home for the next 5 days. On the 5th day, early morning, you will have to take bath and...," he paused.

"And then I will be taken to the gallow where I will be hanged till death," I completed Ali's statement. Ali and I looked at each other and smiled.

"Aaryan, do you need any help from my side?" asked Ali, locking my cell.

"Sir, I want two pens and a thick notebook," I said.

"Ok. But what will you do with them?" questioned Ali.

"I want to write my story. The story of my love and friendship. I want everyone to experience the cost of love," I said holding the bars. Ali raised his eyebrows in surprise and said, "People who end up in this cell, spend most of their time either crying or begging for mercy. You are the first one who wants to write."

"May be I am the first one who has no guilt about his deed. I don't need to cry and God is with me, forever!" he said.

"Ok. You will receive it in an hour. I will leave now for patrolling," assured Ali and went.

The cell was at a very isolated place. I could not see any other prisoners.

Perhaps, I was the only one who was sentenced to death penalty. There was a small vent through which I could peek at the gallow where I had to go after 5 days. That area looked dark, even during the day because of a huge banyan tree in its vicinity. I looked at the gallow and smiled. I was not afraid of dying; I was waiting for it.

There was an earthen pot filled with water, placed in one corner, a black-colored woollen blanket for warmth because of the cold winter nights. An Indian toilet, at one of the corner, though looked clean but was damaged.

Perhaps, the cell had not witnessed any prisoner, for a long time.

"Here are the pens and notebook you asked for," said the guard and slid the covered packet.

"Thanks," I said. He looked at me with a grin and left.

I removed the cover and took out the notebook and pens. I took the pen in my hand and started rubbing it in between my fingers, while I engaged myself to plan, how will I write my story, from where should I start? All such questions occupied my mind just like a debutant author. And for me, it was my first and the last novel.

I gave it a thought and prayed to God to give me strength for another five days, so that I could complete my story.

This is not just a prisoner's story; it is about my life, my love and my reasons to kill Himanshu Joshi.

I was not a criminal; I was a common man; working in Delhi for an IT firm as a software engineer, living happily with my best friend, Nikhil, and in love with my soul mate, Aarushi.

Chapter-2
Day-1
Love at first Sight!

* * *

"Khhuda ki naayab hunar pe yakeen hogaya
Aapke aane bhar se hi mausam haseen ho gaya
Aaj tak jis dil ko apna samajhte the..
Uss dil ki bewafaai pe aaj yakeen hogaya"

I expressed my feelings in a loud tone, when I saw her for the first time, on the adjacent building's terrace. Dressed in a yellow suit with a white dupatta overhead, she looked amazingly beautiful. Her arms were filled with colorful bangles, eyes were lined with kajal and lips were just natural, pink and glossy. Strands of her hair were disturbing the peace of her beautifully carved face. Just a glance of hers would have made one feel blessed.

She looked back at me, with shrunken eyebrows. Her friends too made some *go-to-hell* kind of gestures.

"Get lost," she yelled and raised her hands in air to show her frustration. Typical girls!

"Fine, now I am lost," I said covering my face with a towel. I raised my hand in air and yelled "I don't know, if I should say this or not, but I feel like saying, I Love youuuuuuu!,"

I bet, it was loud enough to reach everyone in the locality. But I hardly cared. I had no reasons as to why I expressed my love. But, at that moment, my feeling was so strong that I could not come out of it. I wanted it to be expressed. Perhaps it was her eternal beauty which stroke my vocal chords, and thus the most exploited, widely and frequently used three words sentence, I love you, came out.

"Do you want me to call the police?" I heard a very different voice. It was definitely not hers. I removed the towel to see who said that.

An aged woman, around 40-45 years or more, dark complexion, big face, wrapped in a blue sari, was standing with one of her arms over the waist and one pressing some numbers over the mobile. Her physical structure proved that even God has lots of work pressure. She was indeed a last minute delivery case.

All the females were staring at me as if they would jump over the terrace, torn me into pieces and drink my blood.

"Girls, you all can go. I will talk to him."

"Ok warden, but warn him so that he never dares to do this again," said one of the girls. All the girls, along with my brand new girlfriend, left the terrace.

Yeah, you read it right, "girlfriend"! We guys can make relationships with the drop of a hat. If we see a beautiful girl, she automatically becomes our girlfriend, and if we talk to a girl, she becomes 'Bhabhi' for our close friends, and if we get hurt, then the cycle continues until, our parents find a girl, suitable for the family and get us married.

I looked at her for a couple of seconds and then pulled out a cigarette from my pocket and placed it in between my lips. Searched for the lighter while she again threatened me, "Shall I call the police?"

"No thanks! I found it!" I said raising the lighter. What annoyed her most was my killing smile.

"This is the last warning to you. If I get another complaint, you will end up behind the bars," warned the lady Hitler and left. She slammed the terrace door to express her anger. As soon as she left, I leaned down to have a glance of my love, but she was nowhere. Depressed, I stepped down to my room.

"So, warmed your eyes?" asked my buddy Nikhil. He was my childhood friend. We always lived together since our days in diapers. Our friendship was so strong that Nikhil tore his IIT results, just to take admission with me in a normal engineering college. He ranked 32 in IIT entrance exam. He could have easily gone in any of the IITs, but he opted to stay with me. I still love him more than my life.

"Yes bro! But later, a wired woman came to nail my eyes," I said jumping over the bed.

"She is the warden. Be aware of her. I am warning you," said Nikhil.

"How do you know her," I asked adjusting the pillow.

"She has a good connection with the local MLA here. I have seen her many times going out with Himanshu Joshi, the MLA's son," replied Nikhil, putting weight on the last two words.

"Who cares? I am just worried about your bhabhi (sister-in-law)," I said with a smile. Remember the relationship cycle I discussed before.

"Ha ha... so you are still searching for my bhabhi

in this girls hostel," said Nikhil, and tossed a bottle of beer.

"Bro, you won't believe. I saw an amazingly beautiful girl today at the terrace," I said opening the beer.

"Really, what was her name?" asked Nikhil putting down his bottle.

"I don't know what she is called now, but within a year she will be Mrs Rathod," I said in a very firm tone, looking straight into Nikhil's eyes.

"I have heard this name for more than hundred times in my life. This may hurt you, but you can't do anything more than placing "Mrs" as prefix before your surname," said Nikhil making faces.

"I bet. I am having a strong feeling that I love her," I just said. I had a habit of making nonsense bets.

"Idiot, stop behaving like a kid. Love is not your cup of coffee," said Nikhil.

"I don't drink coffee. And moreover, love is my mug of beer! You say, are you ready to make a bet," I said extending my hand towards Nikhil.

"But bet on what?" asked Nikhil searching the bottle opener.

"She will be mine one day!" I said kissing my beer bottle.

"In that case, I am ready," smiled Nikhil and threw the opener to me.

He slapped on my palm and said "Bet!"

"If you lose, you are going to sponsor my honeymoon trip when I get married," continued Nikhil.

"And if you win, then," said Nikhil and looked at me.

"Then you will have to fulfill my one wish, which can be anything," I said.

"Ok done! Unless you ask for my wife," said Nikhil and we did cheers once again.

We used to stay at a rented house in Sector 19, Noida. We owned a second hand bike, which we bought from our savings.

Nikhil and I were working in a reputed IT firm in Noida for the past three years. It was our first job, but somehow, I was not satisfied with it. I was just doing it for the sake of my livelihood.

Nikhil was a computer geek, so he loved what he was doing. He would happily spend his entire life hitting keyboards to write some codes. I was completely opposite. I was still counting the number of languages a computer could understand, I infact still wonder as to why did I do computer science engineering. In simple terms, I hated coding.

I always wanted to be a defense officer. Stars on their shoulders, aviator goggles on their eyes, a discipline on their face and the respect they earn in society, always fascinated me. So, I kept filling those never ending defense forms and applying for my dream job. But unfortunately, I never made it through.

I had a habit of expressing my feelings in '*shayaris*'. Perhaps, that was one reason why girls used to hate me.

Why they hated Nikhil, is neither something Nikhil cared about nor I!

Chapter-3
The second meet

* * *

"*Salim, 20 plate aalu paratha laga de* (Salim, prepare twenty aalu parthas)," I placed my order at the road side hotel opposite to our apartment. Salim was the owner of the hotel. He was a great fan of Bollywood superstar, Salman Khan. He used to wear similar bracelets, hanged a duplicate Ray-ban sun glass behind his skin-tight t-shirt and wore a pair of ripped jeans, revealing his hairy legs. The only thing he missed, apart from the looks, was his muscles.

"*Chalo bachaa log, sab line se beth jao* (Come on kids, sit for the breakfast)," I said to small kids whom we used to feed breakfast every Sunday. They were the kids of daily wage workers, who used to work at a construction site near our house.

From the past three months, Nikhil and I got involved with them. We used to teach them during the weekends as well as sponsor their one-time meal. They had become our family, a weekend-family. They used to call us

"*Bhaiya*" (elder brother).

All of them took their plates and sat on the chair. Their eyes talked a lot, and lips remained silent. Unlike every kid, they were not privileged. Looking at their smiling face was enough to make our day.

"Four plates *Aalu paratha* parcel," said a girl. She was from the girls' hostel. She looked at me and passed a very sarcastic smile. I could not digest that gesture.

"Did you make that silly face on me or is it the way you smile?" I asked folding my sleeves. Nikhil completely ignored us. Like all best friends, he would never intervene until I would make things worse. He kept himself occupied with kids.

"Just to remind you, I belong to the same hostel, whose warden threatened you recently," she said raising her eyebrows and then turned to her other co-conspirator. The other girl passed a crafty smile and then they gave each other a high-five. Perhaps they were saying "We did it!"

I didn't feel insulted by her words, but the shrewd smile of another girl accompanying her, ruined the peace of my heart. And moreover, now there was another guy who was keenly interested in knowing the incident; he was Salim.

"Threatened? Really? Do you think that was threatening?" I said. She was really pissed off. She took her parcel and left.

"By the way, can you tell me your friend's name? Are you her roommate?" I asked, knowing that she won't answer.

"Have you seen your face in the mirror?" she said in anger. I smiled as this was the usual comment I have been hearing since childhood.

"And moreover, that was not proposal, but a shameless act," she continued giving the lecture, "Neither she is interested in you nor I am interested in telling you her name. So just...," she said and left with her parcel, showing me her middle finger.

I stood quite, didn't reply anything for her act.

"*Sale, jawaab de*, since morning you are getting insulted!" screamed Nikhil, after seeing me quite.

I raised my hand and said, "See there." My girl was standing at the gallery dressed in a white salwar and pink top. She looked amazingly beautiful. She was drying her hair with a pink towel. Her innocent face was so pleasant, that I was left speechless.

"Kisi roz tere dil ki darwaze mei dastak denge,
Aaj is oor khade hai, ek din tere rooh mei honge."

My tone was loud enough to vibrate the peace around her ears. She looked at me, actually stared, and then upstretched her hands in air to express her feelings. Feelings of frustration!

"*Bhaiya woh ladki kaun hai*?" asked Raju, one among the kids.

My girl heard that. She was dazed and then eyed at me, waiting for my response. I didn't say a word, just kept gazing at her with a smile.

"She is your *Bhabhi*! Aaryan's wife!" snickered Nikhil.

"Say Namaste to Bhabhi," continued Nikhil. I was smiling like an idiot. Somewhere, I too wanted kids to shout, *Bhabhi*!

"*Namaste Bhabhiiiiiiiiiii*!" shouted all the kids in chorus. I was stunned; and so was she. Her eyes popped out and she furiously stared at me.

"I didn't ask them to say so," I yelled.

"I am going to log a complaint against you," she screamed back and left the gallery.

"*Kamine*, because of you she left," I kicked Nikhil.

"Ya right! As if she came out to see you," Nikhil taunted back and sat down on the chair and started eating his breakfast.

I too joined them for breakfast. Still unsure about love, but somewhere beneath my heart, I used to feel happy whenever she graced me with her appearance. Perhaps that small happiness is what you call the seed of love. Now, I too had that love seed, sowed in my fragile heart.

That night, I couldn't resist myself from penning down my feelings for her in my personal diary.

"*I am her shadow, I will always follow her*
I will always pray that she never goes away from me
My feelings are attached to her
My life is devoted to her,
I overlooked the beauty of the world when I saw her,
I don't know if she is my destiny, or
Just a lesson in life..."

Chapter 4
"First Break-Up!!"

* * *

"Aaryan, there is a post for you," called Harish from the administration department. I was in office, getting bugged by the bugs in software. Yes, like most of the software engineers, half of my day would go in fixing the bugs and the other half would go in fighting with QA engineers, whose success depend upon how much bug they find in a software we built.

Newton's first law of motion is applicable in software industries too.

"A bug can never be created nor be destroyed; it can only be transferred from one code to another."

Our manager, Mihir Jaiswal, was no less than a Dracula. The only difference I could tell is, Dracula used teeth to suck blood, but Mihir, being in software industry, used Wi-Fi, outlook, and meetings to suck our blood. In case if you are trying to imagine his physical structure, then let me stop you right there. His eyebrows always raised, lips twisted towards left, hands bent like a kangaroo, and legs as thin as an ostrich's legs. Yes, he was an animal.

"Ok, I am coming to collect it," I said and kept the phone down.

"*Chal neeche* (lets go down)," I said to Nikhil. He used to sit right next to me.

"What happened?" asked Nikhil, typing hard at keyboards to write a robust code.

"Let's go and smoke," I replied, tugging my shirt in.

Newton's second law of motion also applies here in IT.

"A software engineer typing codes, will remain hitting keyboard until and unless he is offered a cigarette by his close friend."

"Done, let's move," said Nikhil and locked his system. We grabbed a cup of cappuccino and left the coding premises.

"Hey, I need to collect a post," I told him.

"Post? Did she send you a love letter?" asked Nikhil sarcastically.

"That day is not far," I replied patting Nikhil's back. We reached the administration cell located at the ground floor.

"Harish Sir, my post?" I asked taking a sip of my coffee.

"*Yeh lo jee* (take it)," said Harish passing me the post.

"*Sarkari office ka post lag raha hai,* (It looks like a government office letter)," continued Harish showing his interest in my letter.

I looked at the post, raised my eyebrows, stared at Harish and said, "It is from the HRD."

Harish stood paralyzed. It was not the HRD which caused that trauma, but the expression over my face.

"You know *Mihir Jaiswal*?" asked Nikhil putting his hand over Harish's shoulders. Harish gazed at Nikhil. Still puzzled.

Harish nodded his head to say, yes.

"He is found guilty of harassing two engineers," I whispered.

"What harassment? Mental?" asked Harish in vibrating tone

"No, the second type," replied Nikhil, moving his trousers zip up and down. I felt like laughing loud. I pressed my lips with my teeth and made a serious face.

Harish's eyes popped out and he stood stagnant with his mouth wide opened.

Nikhil and I took another sip of our coffee and left the scene. Since that day, Harish looked very cautious and scared. Whenever he used to see Mihir in parking or in office, he would hide himself behind the desks or conceal his assets with files. Mihir too was surprised with that behavior, but he never bothered to investigate that.

"Let me see the post now," I said taking the parcel out of my pocket.

Meanwhile, Nikhil lightened the cigarette and came closer to have a look.

"Dude, your exam is on next Saturday," said Nikhil after going through the letter.

It was an admit card for the Combined Defense Services Exams. I had applied for it. Just by reading the letter, I could imagine myself in an officer's attire, with aviator goggles over my eyes, and girls tossing flying kisses to me.

"Yes, now I will have to prepare myself for the exams," I said taking a puff.

"And what about the girl next door?" asked Nikhil with a cunning smile over his face.

"You need not work hard to get loved… just work out your heart," I narrated a classy dialogue, which was well appreciated by Nikhil.

Then I spent the whole day in office doing something that I was not born for; writing codes. Soon, the office hour was over and we happily packed our bags to make a move.

"Let's go and collect beer," said Nikhil kicking his bike.

"Rascal, I have exams next Saturday," I yelled while sitting at the pillion.

"It is still eight days to go. In eight days, if earth can rotate eight times, then you are just a tiny human, why are you worried? You can easily prepare in a day," explained Nikhil. This is the problem with engineers. No matter how burning the situation is, they will always wait till the last moment to prepare for the fight.

"Hmmm… right. Let's enjoy tonight," I said gladly, as I believe, foolish would be the one who would deny a chilled beer against an exam preparations.

We stopped near a bar shop and filled our office bag with a carat of chilled beer and drove back to our room.

"Bhai, let's drink on terrace today," I proposed to Nikhil. It was the end of March, and so the weather was getting a bit hotter during days. But, fortunately nights were pleasant and hence, I thought of having beer under the moonlight.

He made some weird face initially, but finally he felt prey to my innocent face and agreed. We packed some snacks and placed all the beer bottles inside the ice container.

"A guy can live without a hot girl but can never compromise with a chilled beer," said Nikhil while carefully placing the bottles inside the container.

We mounted over the water tank and placed all the stuffs. The weather also changed itself to please our mood.

Cold breeze and cloudy sky!

Nikhil couldn't wait longer and he took out two bottles and passed one to me. "To the ...," said Nikhil raising his bottle of beer.

"To the girl next building, Cheers," I completed.

We drank half of our stock without taking a break. The night was getting high and so was the beer. After having three bottles each, we gave ourselves a short break and laid down facing towards the sky. Cold breeze touched our faces; moon struggling to find a way out of the dark clouds and a deep silence made everything so beautiful.

"Dude, why it says, "Smoking is injurious to health"...whereas, the recent survey says, it is love that has claimed more life paralleled to anything else," I waffled lightning a cigarette.

"What's your point?" asked Nikhil raising his eyebrows to confirm his confused state.

"If the government really wants to save lives, then why only cigarette packs and other nicotine items have that warning message.

They should also mention "Love is injurious to health. It may lead to suicide, murder, rape, and acid attack etc, " on every soft toys, hearts, and valentine greetings?" I raised my genuine concern.

"You are correct. *Government ne yaha bhi game khel diya. (*Government played its game here as well*),*" agreed Nikhil while sitting up in excitement.

We were all set to re-start the party, when someone opened the grill of the opposite terrace. It was dark and so we could not see the face. But they were girls, as we could hear their voice.

"Such a romantic weather," screamed one of the girls in the group.

I don't know what was so romantic in the weather

and moreover, why are girls so obsessed with romance. For us, the weather was just perfect to get drunk.

"Really, we could have missed it if Aarushi would not have informed us," said another girl.

Nikhil and I crawled slowly towards the end of the tank to hear tones more evidently. We narrowed our eyes to penetrate our sight inside the darkness to get a view. We were unable to figure out any face until, someone switched on the terrace light.

"Why did you switch on the light?" screamed a girl.

Nikhil and I hardly bothered to get caught as some of the light rays also fell on us.

"*Bhai, inme se bhabhi kaun si hai* (Who among these, is my sister-in-law)," poked Nikhil.

I rubbed my eyes to get a clear view. I started scanning from one end to the other, before my search ended at a beautiful girl dressed in a black *churidaar* and a pink top. Hair completely messed up, but yet, making her look gorgeous. Due to the raised alcoholic level in my veins, my eyes were unable to catch other details over her face. But no doubt, she was looked beautiful.

"Hello!" I stood up and yelled. Nikhil pinched my leg and asked me to sit.

The peace at the next terrace was disturbed by my "Hello". Girls tried hard to figure me out. Suddenly someone said,

"I think he is the same guy,"

"Yes, I am the same guy," I said raising my toast.

"Is he drunk? Let's call the warden," suggested a girl dressed in a yellow suit. Swear on God, as soon as I heard, "warden", half of my senses returned back. She was horrible, indeed!

"No. Stop," said my love and walked towards the

railing. She tugged the strands of her hair behind her ears and stared at me.

"I don't care who you are, but I know one thing, you are the cheapest, most idiot and stupid guy I have ever seen. This shows your upbringing," she said in a very loud tone.

I just stood paralyzed. Never ever in my life, I had heard those words. I could have equally insulted her, but perhaps it was my upbringing, which stopped me. I knew, she didn't like the way I used to express myself, but what she did was equally insulting to me.

"Hello, whoever you are, I don't care. But just shut up and dare not say a single word again. You don't know him; he is an idiot who loves you madly," said Nikhil, angrily, pointing finger at my love. I knew he was lying, as he had seen me falling in love many a times. But, he also knew, I had never expressed my love for anyone before.

"I think we should log a complaint against them," proposed one of the girls among them.

"You are right, we should," chorused other girls and made a move.

"I love you. I don't know why I do so, but, I do," I said and then took a pause to gulp another sip of beer. Everyone at the opposite terrace, stopped.

"No matter how cheap you think I am, but my love is pure and honest. Yes, I agree, I am not that yo-yo type of guy who has a very pleasant personality to impress beauties like you, but I have a clean heart that includes you in all its wishes. I am not an expert who knows to gel beautiful words and express love, but I am not a flirty guy.

I am not cheap, just mad for you. I live with dignity and love with honesty. You don't know about me, so stop judging me," I said, but this time, my eyes were moist.

I looked at Nikhil and said, "*Bhai*, I am not cheap,"

"Leave her *yaar*. She doesn't deserve you," shouted

Nikhil pulling me down.

"Let's go to our rooms. We are unfortunate to have these kind of idiots as our neighbours," said a girl among them. Listening to her command, all girls made a move to the downstairs.

"Hey you, pink top," I yelled while she was locking the terrace grill.

"Let me tell you something before you leave. I know you are beautiful ...lovely... You are the nerve which connects my heart to brain. May be that is the reason, my heart skips a beat and brain gets paralyzed whenever I adore you. I am ready to sacrifice everything it takes to pay the cost of love, but not my dignity. It's over. And one thing more, I am not cheap," I said looking at her. She stood there for a couple of seconds and then left.

Like all my previous love stories, this one also ended up very soon. What made me so mad for her? How could I say, I was in love, when even I wasn't sure about it? That time, I didn't have an answer for it, but today, I have.

The aura of her blissful presence, the silence and simplicity over her face, the sparkling shine over her glossy pink lips, the colorful bangles in her arms, and the stud on her nose, together played a conspiracy and hijacked my heart.

I don't remember where I read, but girls do like guys who express themselves. But an Indian guy can yell and let the whole world know whom he hates, but when it comes to express his love, he can't even tell to the one, he loves.

Chapter 5
"I know her name"

* * *

It was more than a week, I watched her. I kept myself engaged with my exam preparations and convinced myself not to see her. It was like blending in against my will. But I had decided, no matter what, I was not running to see her until she says sorry to me. I knew how stupid it was. Why she would say sorry, if this was what she wished. But, if you love somebody, you always want him or her to come back, hold your arms, look into your eyes and say nothing. Because, in love, it's not tongue, only eyes which speaks.

Examination day arrived. Like most of the examinee, I too took bath and did prayer before leaving for the examinations. I called up my parents to seek their blessings. I knew they would spend the whole day praying and bribing god.

"Hello Ma. *Namaste!* I have my exam today. Pray for me," I called up my mother.

"Don't worry beta, you will clear the exams. God

will take care," said my mother. Typical Indian mothers and the way they use God's name in their discussion would leave you in doubts if they have any direct contact with God.

"Okay, now it's time to go. Talk to you later, bye," I said.

"Take care. *Jeete raho* (have a long life)," said mom and hung up the call.

"Dude, are you ready to crack the exam?" asked Nikhil dressing his hair in the side mirror of his bike.

"*Bhag sale, gaadi start kar* (Shut up rascal; start the bike),"I said placing myself at the pillion.

Nikhil dropped me at the examination centre. There were hundreds of examinees, some standing with their group of acquaintances and some fighting to see their roll numbers on the notice board. It is always fun to visualize the environment at examination centers. You would notice four different types of species at every examination centre. First are the spiritual species. They would pray to every God, contribute money to beggars, keep on kissing their sacred bands or chains, and chant some holy words.

Second species are those who are the last minute fighters. They are normally found sitting at a less noisy place, with their index finger inside their ears and just mugging every single word of the book.

Third species are likewise known as mobile lovers. They are mostly found scattered with their mobile phones. And the last species are the ones who fill the form just for the sake of giving it a try. They are the ones, who come at the examination centre to see new faces, make new acquaintances and try their luck. They are usually found flipping coins to answer objective type questions. They are also the ones who spend most of the exam time in staring the ceiling for an answer. I belonged to the fourth species.

"Now! Get ready to be an officer's friend," I said

placing aviator glasses over my eyes.

"Bro, it really suits you. You know, I really want you to get selected. I will be the first person to salute you," wished Nikhil hugging me tight.

"Thanks bro. It is my dream, I am not going to miss this," I said patting his back.

"Yep. All the best," said Nikhil and started his bike.

"Catch you soon," I said and left towards notice board to find my roll number.

"Jai Hind, officer Aaryan Rathod," someone yelled.

I turned back and found Nikhil waving his hands in the air while driving the wheel. Idiot, he made me embarrassed, but at the same time it brought a lofty and confident smile over my face.

Everyone who heard it thought, there was an officer among the crowd, so they all stood consciously while I stepped inside the campus with a proud smile over my face.

"Excuse me, where is room number 102?" I asked one of the volunteers.

"Go straight, take first right," he replied and wished me luck.

I prayed to God before entering inside the room. It is very much business as usual. No matter how much you prepare yourself, you will always call for God to help you out.

My roll number was pasted at the second last bench. There were mostly boys in the room. I looked at them and smiled, but no one bothered to smile back. I completely ignored them and occupied my place. I was simply looking around at other examinees, some were just laying down on their desk, some were perhaps mugging up general knowledge and some were sitting at the last bench watching something on their mobile phone. A sarcastic smile on their facial expression made me doubt if they were watching something nasty on their phones. I would have loved to join them, but at that time, I was looking at myself as a future officer. So that was nothing less than a stupidity to me.

I was in my mental peace when all of a sudden a girl entered the exam room. No, she was not my beloved, but her friend. She was the one who suggested to file a complaint against me.

"God, has she come with police?" I whispered slowly to myself. I tried to hide my face with my palms.

But some girls are real vultures. They can catch anything from any distance. She looked at me with shrunken eyebrows. I was stunned to witness her and so was she. I avoided her and looked outside the window. But, God had some more weird plans for me. Her seat was right in front of me.

"God, I didn't pray to you for this. Stop giving me bizarre surprises!" I looked at the sky and begged God. All general knowledge, formulae, chemical reactions that I had learned, vaporized.

Boys at the last bench now had something more worth watching. Yes, she was beautiful enough to capture attention. I hardly bothered about it.

"Camera on kar (switch on the camera)," whispered one of the guys sitting in the back.

"Zoom it," said someone among them. I turned back to see what was happening. They kept their mobile down at the desk and looked uneasy when I caught them. I knew they were attempting to take a picture of that girl.

I didn't tell them anything and turned. I noticed that a strap of her bra was visible along her shoulder. Now I knew what those guys were trying to seize. I had three options that time, firstly hit those guys, secondly, just avoid and lastly, tell the girl. But, I gave the idea to hit those guys as it might have led to my disqualification to write the exam, and simply avoiding was something a future officer and a real man can't afford to do.

I knew if I tried to say anything to her, she would ultimately end up blaming me. But I had no other option than to tell her. I moved out of my desk and stood in front of hers.

"I need to talk to you for a minute," I said. She looked at me, angrily. I had my fingers crossed anyway. Superstitious, I know, but I was just praying she doesn't insult me at that place.

"Say," she said

"Not here. Let's go to the corridor. Please," I folded my hand and requested her. She felt pity on me and stood up to come out.

"Look, if you are trying to ask me anything stupid or going to say sorry for that night, I am not at all interested," she said pointing fingers at me.

I looked around to notice that how many fellow examinees were looking at us. It was quite embarrassing really.

"Go to washroom, and watch your dress. You have not seen cheap guys yet," I said looking straight in her eyes.

She looked at her shoulder and realized what I meant. Hiding her strap inside the suit she looked at those guys in the last bench. She understood everything.

I left her there, and came inside the room. Those guys were looking at me with anger. I simply smiled and sat at my desk.

"Thanks," she said after returning back from the washroom.

I just nodded my head and then she turned back.

Soon, the exam started and it went very good. I struggled with general knowledge as I never bothered about who Babur was and when was he born or who was our last governor general. Rest all, was a cakewalk for me.

Nikhil was waiting outside the centre to pick me up. He called me.

"Hey, come out fast. There are lots of beauties here," said Nikhil over the phone.

"*Kamine, tu ladki taad raha hai* (Idiot, you are watching girls!)" I replied walking towards the exit gate.

"*Bhai,* was this CDS exam or Miss India contest? I am also going to appear for this exam next time," said Nikhil. I could feel the excitement in his voice.

"Why to fill form for just appearing? You can just colour the dates on your calendar and visit examination centres," I replied.

"Excuse me," said someone.

I looked around to see if that was for me.

"Hi, I am Swati," she said. Yes, she was my neighbour, whom I saved a few hours back from going viral over the internet.

"*Sale,* who is this girl? Are you talking to a girl?," asked Nikhil over phone.

"Just a minute bro," I replied to Nikhil and looked at Swati.

"Yes, say," I replied her. Trust me, I was scared.

"I am sorry," she said in a very soft tone.

"It's alright. I have no grudges against you," I replied.

"We are girls, and we are always worried about our security. And the way you always looked at her, made us a bit mad and concerned," she explained.

"But today what you did, proves that, you are not among those boys, who can harm a girl," she continued.

"Do you really love her?" she asked a question whose reply was known to every cell of my body.

"Yes I do. I still do. No matter how much I tried to ignore her for the past few days, but I always started my day by thinking of her smiling face, and ended it with a dream of having her in my life one day. But, now I am not going to trouble her anymore," I replied though I was still unsure about my last statement.

Swati had a smile on her face. She punched me on my arms and said, "You will get her one day. I promise you."

"That's ok, but why did you hit me," I said with a sarcastic smile holding my arms. She laughed and extended her hand for a hand shake.

"By the way, I didn't ask your name yet," said Swati.

"I am Aaryan and my best friend, who is going to kill me when I go out, is Nikhil," I said pointing her to my mobile phone. Nikhil was still on the call and he had heard everything.

"Do you want to ask me something before we leave?" asked Swati

I showed her my palm and said, "This line that you see here over my palm is the line of my soul mate, my life, my love. I just wanted to know the name of this line."

"Oh.... Ok... I got it!! So this line is called," she paused and looked at me, smiled and said, "Aarushi."

I can't express the feeling I had at that moment. Just knowing the name of my love was like a biggest success for me. I was on cloud nine. I wanted to shout out loud and make the whole world hear the name of my love. A strange but heavenly feeling was there in my heart. Every cell of my body was saying just one thing, "I love you Aarushi, I love you Aarushi."

* * *

"You have not eaten anything yet?" asked a guard who was on his night duty.

"What will happen if I don't eat?" I asked refilling my pen.

"You will die," he replied.

"I am going to die anyway in next four days. So how is your food going to change my destiny?" I said stretching my legs. I had been continuously writing for eight hours now.

"Is writing going to change your destiny?" he asked pointing towards the pages I wrote.

"Not my destiny, but it may make someone revisit the law book and bring some amendments," I replied looking at him.

"God knows what you are writing. Anyway, we are going to switch off the lights. So go to sleep," he said and left. After a few minutes the lights were off. A lamppost, at some fifty-meter distance opposite to my cell was the only source of light at night. There was a deep silence around. Though there was silence in the air, but there was a lot of noise within me whuch reminded me of my loneliness, my losses and my helplessness.

I kept all the pages aside and lay over the mat. I took Aarushi's photo out from my shirt pocket and looked at her. I remember, I took this pic of hers when she came to say, "I am sorry Aaryan". She looked cute and innocent. She was dressed in her favourite blue color churidar salwar suit. White dupatta covering her head, colorful bangles swinging on her wrists, a blue bindi at the center of kajal lined beautiful eyes just made her look perfect.

God knows when my tired eyes gave up and I slept, but my dreams were dedicated to Aarushi.

Chapter 6
Day 2

* * *

It was 5:00 am in the morning when the alarm buzzed to wake up all the prisoners. I woke up and stretched my body. It was a cold morning. I rolled my blanket and placed it at a corner. Sun was playing hide and seek with the clouds. I looked through the vent to have a glimpse of the gallon. There was a grave silence, even birds refused to chirp there. I looked at the hanging rope which was as alone as me and said "Four days more, I am coming to give you company".

I picked Aarushi's photo and kissed her. The smile on her face was genuinely sweet with a perfect blend of shyness.

"Aarushi, you know, I feel very lonely here. No one comes to talk to me, and this rope you see there, behind that banyan tree, is the only one, which has no company, just like me. But after four days, that rope and I will hang out together. And then I will see you from the heaven, if I end up there. Now, it's time to take bath, will catch you later." I said while looking at Aarushi's photo and then placed it under my blanket. I took bath at the nearby well and changed my dress.

Now, I was all set to start my writing again.

Chapter 7

"He is not that bad!!"

* * *

"Salim bhai, I need to ask you something about Aaryan," enquired Swati to Salim. Salim looked at her surprisingly and asked her to grab a chair.

Swati took a corner seat.

"Yes madam, first of all have this masala tea," said Salim and offered a cup of tea to Swati. Salim's masala tea was indeed the best in the city. God knows what magical powder he used to put in it.

Swati took a sip and said "Wow!! *Bhaiya* it's really awesome and refreshing." She took one more.

"Aaryan also loves my masala tea," said Salim while sitting on the opposite chair.

"Can you tell me something more about Aaryan?"

"Why do you want to know about him?" asked Salim

"I am a bit confused about his personality. Sometimes we feel, he is totally an idiot and irritating and sometimes he is completely different," explained Swati.

"Okay, you mean, you don't like the way he expresses his love for your friend," said Salim with a cynical smile on his face.

"You also know about this," asked Swati shockingly.

"Whenever he has to see your friend, he would come to my shop and drink masala tea for hours. I think he really likes her," replied Salim with an over-confident smile on his face.

"I don't know. These days, guys just flirt. There is no more love..."

"May be you are right, but Aaryan is a bit different. He is a very emotional guy," said Salim while narrowing his eyes to show an emotional side of him.

"For how long do you know him?" asked Swati while taking a sip from her cup.

"I think, it has been more than three years now," said Salim.

"Was he like this before? I mean, does he tease every other girl on street?" whispered Swati, seeing a few customers at the shop.

"No – no – no – no, never," said Salim nodding his head. "This is the first time he is behaving like this. I think he has really got some feelings for your friend," explained Salim.

"I am not sure. My friend, Aarushi, is a very common girl. She comes from a middle class family. Her dad and younger brother died when she was just five years old. Her mother is a tailor and lives in Lucknow in UP. Aarushi is preparing for IAS mains, and I am pretty sure that she would make it through," narrated Swati.

"And that's the reason I don't want her to get into any trouble. She is very simple Salim bhai," said Swati. She looked concerned about Aarushi.

"As far as I know Aaryan, he is not what you are

thinking. You might have seen some children coming to my shop during the weekend. They are children of the daily wageworkers working at the construction site. Aaryan sponsors their lunch. He is very soft and emotional person," justified Salim.

"Thanks Salim *bhai*. I too feel he is not that bad. But the way he projects himself is really irritating," giggled Swati. Salim too laughed and said, "You are right madam. Sometimes he is."

"Would you mind if I ask Aaryan's mobile number?" asked Swati. Salim thought for a while and then passed my number to her.

"Thanks" said Swati and left for the hostel after having the free tea.

Next day, when I went to Salim's shop, he narrated everything about the secret enquiry. I was glad at least someone was trying to know about me. Salim also told me about Aarushi and her family background.

"Are you crying?" asked Salim

"No, it's dust," I said wiping my eyes. Somewhere I thought, I was not doing it right way. I can love her, I can admire her, but that doesn't mean I should make it so public. I had guilt somewhere in my heart.

"Aaryan, if you don't mind, can I suggest you something?" said Salim, placing his hand over my shoulder.

"Yes, Salim *bhai*. But if you want me to forget her, then please don't say it," I said. Mostly when your love story gets screwed, all your near and dear ones suggest you to forget it and start fresh.

I knew, mine too was screwed up, but I wanted to make things right. I wasn't ready to give up.

"No, I am not saying to forget her, but first let her know about you. She must understand you before she commits to you. Girls are emotional. If they love, they commit, unlike boys. Boys first love, then kiss, then sleep, then they get so bored up that they just leave for the next prey," said Salim.

He was correct. Love has certainly lost its meaning. It has become the most exploited word.

"You are right. But I am not among those boys. I really love her. Tell me what should I do? I just don't want to lose her," I said.

"First try to be friends with her. Interact with her, know her likes, dislikes, spend some time, and give her some space," said Salim. He sounded like a love guru.

"May be you are right. But how will I ever approach her to become my friend?" I definitely sounded like a novice.

"If your love is true, then *Allah* will surely help you out. You need not worry," said Salim with a confident smile on his face.

I looked at him for a second and said, "Why are you wasting time in making tea and *paratha*? You should join Delhi University as *Loveology* professor!". Salim laughed loudly and then we raised a toast – tea!

That night, I narrated the whole story to Nikhil. He too felt sad for Aarushi and advised me to follow what Salim suggested. Unlike most friends, he didn't ask me to forget her, but said, "Bro, now if you ever dare to forget her and look for some other girl, I am going to kick you real hard."

"What do you think, where will all these things end, I mean my love story?" I asked him offering a cigarette. Yes, that was a bribe to get a favourable answer.

"I don't think you guys will get married. Maximum friendship," said Nikhil exhaling the nicotine gas out of his nose. I really wanted to take that cigarette back; the answer was indeed not favourable.

"We will get married. I bet you," I said and extended my hand. Nikhil looked at me for a few seconds and said,

"*Chal* Bet!"

"You rascal, I love her truly, and this is known to every cell of my body," I said taking a puff.

"You are an idiot. And everyone in this colony knows this. Moreover, you don't even understand what love means. It requires blind trust on your partner. And trust is too tough for you to understand," said Nikhil. After listening to his arrogant reply, I silently prayed to God to give him a heartache.

"Maine aksar logo ko mandiro mein sar jhukate dekha hai,

Bata kaun hai yaha, jisne khuda dekha hai" I replied. "They all bow their head in front of God. Have you ever worried what makes them do so? That is love, my friend. You may call it blind faith, but let me tell you, faith, if not blind, is not a faith at all. And the same stands true for love."

I said in full attitude. He was speechless for a moment and then left saying, the "*F*" word and throwing the cigarette bud on my face. The very next moment, I vomited all the classic slangs dedicated to his all blood relatives.

Chapter 8
Seriously, I was an Idiot

* * *

It was almost mid-night when Swati thought of initiating a discussion about me with Aarushi. They used to stay awake preparing for their civil services exams. On the other hand, Nikhil and I were hitting hard on our laptop keyboards to fix software bugs. Mihir, our deadly boss, had already warned us twice for not meeting the timeline.

"Aarushi, I wanted to discuss something with you," said Swati while giving head massage to Aarushi.

"Yes say. Why are you being so formal?" said Aarushi playing with her hair clutcher.

"Don't get mad. Just try listening for a few minutes," replied Swati as she knew any discussion about me would make Aarushi furious.

"Okay. I hope you are not going to say something weird."

"This is regarding Aaryan," said Swati.

Aarushi made some strange face and asked, "Who

is he?"

"The guy who looks at you, says shayaris, waits for you at Salim's shop and,"

"And the guy who irritates me a lot," completed Aarushi. She stood up and placed both her hands on her waist to show her frustration. Swati could sense the anger on her face. She preferred being quite.

"How can you even talk about that idiot," asked Aarushi.

"First have a seat. I asked you to listen first and then we can discuss," said Swati, gesturing Aarushi to sit on the chair. Aarushi took a deep breath and then sat beside Swati on the bed.

"Fine, tell me," said Aarushi

Swati shared the examination hall story and her discussion with Salim with Aarushi. It took Swati almost fifteen minutes to narrate the story. Aarushi calmly listened to the whole story and then stood up.

"What happened?" asked Swati. She expected some discussions, but Aarushi looked least interested.

"You wanted me to listen to you. I did. Now what?" asked Aarushi.

"I don't think he is that bad," said Swati.

"So what? I don't care if he is good or bad. I am here to fulfil dreams of my mother. I have no time to even think of him," said Aarushi placing kettle over the gas stove. Swati remained mute for a while and then sat beside Aarushi, watching her making tea.

"Now what?" asked Aarushi

"I feel he is really nice and innocent guy. He will never do anything wrong to you," initiated Swati.

"If he is so nice, then why don't you go ahead with him," said Aarushi sarcastically.

"I wish, I could. But he likes you," said Swati.

"Stop this meaningless topic and have this wonderful tea," said Aarushi offering tea to Swati.

"Okay. Let's see if he really loves you or not. If he is really that honest and innocent," said Swati picking her cell phone.

"You have his number?" asked Aarushi raising her eyebrow to maximum she could.

"Relax. I took it from Salim. And I am doing this for you guys," said Swati searching my number in the contact list.

"I can't believe this," said Aarushi raising her hands out of frustration.

"Wait. I am unable to find his number. I don't remember with what name I saved it," said Swati.

"Aah, here you go! Romeo, nice name huh!" said Swati and looked at Aarushi for a praise. Aarushi looked least interested and took a sip of her tea.

"So what shall I type?" asked Swati.

"Say I love you, and let's get married. And then both of you get married and leave me happily. Nonsense," replied Aarushi arrogantly.

"Nope! I have an idea," said Swati and started hitting her nails over her touch screen cell phone.

"Hi"

My cell phone beeped. I moved my eyeballs to see the message, still typing some JAVA codes. Salim did not tell me that, Swati had taken my cell number from him. Hence, I couldn't guess the messenger's name.

"Whose number is this?" I said, picking up my cell phone. Single guys can forget anything in this world if they get a message from an unknown number, saying 'hi'. The very first thought that strikes them is, "May be this is some girl," it happened to me too.

"Hi, may I know who is this?" I replied. I stood up

from the chair and went to the balcony.

"What happened? Done with the fix?" asked Nikhil

"Nope. I just want to stretch," I replied. Nikhil was hardly bothered and he resumed his coding job.

"*Are you in love?*" another message appeared on my cell phone. I was shocked to read it. Only Nikhil and Salim knew my love story and I was quite sure they wouldn't do it. Salim was a miser. He used to give miss calls if he had to talk to me.

"*May I know who is this?*" I replied. I didn't want to disclose my half cooked love story to everyone.

"*I got this number from one of the astrology website. I have made several impossible love stories successful. Do you want me to guide you?*"

I indeed registered myself on most of the astrology websites to check if my love with Aarushi will be a success or not. Will she fall in love with me or not. Trust me, no matter what degree you hold, there will always be a moment in life when you start believing on every damn cuts on your palm, stars and planet positions. And I was undergoing that moment.

"*Yes I had registered. May I know your name?*" I replied, as I was still interested in knowing the name of the messenger.

"*You should not be bothered about my name. I am an astrologer, who by the grace of God has all the abilities to bring two souls together forever in just 5 days,*" typed Swati. Aarushi was laughing loud as for her it was quite an entertainment and on the other hand, I was getting more serious with every message.

"*How much do you charge?*" I replied, as I wanted to see if it was authentic or someone was trying to con me.

"*I don't ask for fees. You may give whatever you feel and that too after the successful completion,*" replied Swati.

This made me believe it was quite genuine. I thought, I am not going to lose anything if nothing works out after 5 days. I thought of sharing this with Nikhil, but later I dropped the plan as he would call me an insane and ask to stop behaving like an idiot.

"*Fine. What do you want me to do,*" I replied.

After a few minutes, I got another message

"*Send the HD image of your right hand palm. And message me the girl's name,*" texted Swati. Aarushi was enjoying every moment of it.

I read the message and again got confused whether I should really send the image or not. I thought for a while and then the love insect inside my heart won and I decided to take the image. I know, it sounds crazy, but it's equally true that only a crazy guy achieves success.

My cell phone's camera was not at all good. I had an old Chinese phone with not so good camera quality. My dad gifted me this when I got placed in the company. After that, I didn't even think of buying a new model. Nikhil had a decent phone, so I decided to take the snap from his phone.

"Bhai, pass me your phone," I asked Nikhil, who surprisingly was not coding. He was surfing images of various girls on Facebook.

Nikhil looked at me with suspicious eyes and later handed me his cell phone. He warned me not to use for any wrong purpose.

I went near the balcony and started the photography of my palm. I took three to four pictures from all the angles. I didn't want to take chance of missing even a single line on it.

"What the hell are you doing?" asked Nikhil when he saw me performing the photography session with his mobile.

"Nothing. Just testing your cell phone's camera," I

said while sending those pictures to my cell phone.

"But why were you taking pictures of your palm?" questioned Nikhil.

"Just like that," I said and returned him the phone after deleting the images.

"I am quite sure, you are doing something idiotic. I can see that in your face," he said making faces and then returned back to his laptop.

I attached all the images and forwarded it. I was eagerly waiting for a reply.

"Hey see, he has sent his palm images," said Swati opening the attachments.

"Is he really that idiot?" said Aarushi peeking into Swati's cell phone.

"You may think he is an idiot, but he is actually innocent. He is ready to do anything for you," said Swati looking at Aarushi.

"Okay. In that case ask him to pick fresh cow dung tomorrow morning and keep it at the entrance of his flat," said Aarushi challenging Swati's comment on me.

"This is really bad. But I am sure he will do it," said Swati. What the hell was that! Finally, it was me who was getting grinded.

Almost fifteen minutes passed and I didn't receive any message. I decided to make a call.

"Hey, he is calling. What shall I do now?" asked Swati after seeing my call. Aarushi suggested cutting the call, but Swati was afraid that rejecting the call might leave an impression that everything was fake.

"And what we are doing is fake. So cut the call," yelled Aarushi.

"Nope, I will pick it. And you shut up and don't dare to speak a single word," warned Swati, before accepting the call. Finally she picked it up.

"Hello," greeted Swati

"Hi, Aaryan here. I am sorry to call you, but I just sent you the images of my palm and have been waiting for long to get a reply from you," I said politely as I was afraid that she might get angry and ruin the lines of my palm and hence my future.

"Yes I got it. I was having a close look at them, but you didn't mention the girl's name," said Swati. She sounded similar to ladies saint we see in *Sanskar* channel.

"Sorry I forgot. Her name is Aarushi," I said. As the phone was on loudspeaker so Aarushi too heard the conversation. She made faces when I said her name.

"For how long do you know her?"

"It has been more than a month," I said.

"Just a month! Are you serious? Why don't you give yourself time? You may find someone better," suggested Swati "See, if you can help me, I will be very grateful to you, but if you are suggesting me to find a better girl then just forget it and delete those images. I need help not suggestions," I said bluntly.

"I was just testing you. Sorry if you felt bad. Anyway, could you please tell me the date and time of your birth," asked Swati.

"Date of birth is 23rd January 1987. Sorry I don't remember the time. I am pretty sure the maternity ward had a clock but that time, I didn't know how to read it," I replied like an idiot.

"*Hahahahahaa*... You are such a sweetheart," said Swati laughing out loud. Aarushi covered her face with a pillow so that she could laugh liberally without letting me know her attendance. I liked the word, "sweetheart", though.

"Do you know hers?" asked Swati. Indeed it was stupid question from her end.

"I don't. But the love for her took birth inside my

heart on 22nd April 2012 at 9:00 am when I saw her for the first time at her terrace," I said. Swati and Aarushi were shocked to hear the details.

"I like it. Fine, I have some tasks for you. If you complete all the tasks, then I am 99 per cent sure that she will talk to you," said Swati.

"What? She will just talk to me? She has already talked to me twice. First time she called me an idiot and second time cheap. And I am 100 per cent sure that she will talk to me anytime I appear before her. What do you mean by talk? Could you please elaborate the limitations of this, talk," I was frustrated. But the girl's next building had a good laugh listening to my annoyed sound.

"Relax Aaryan. I meant, she would patiently talk and listen to you," explained Swati. Now that was quite acceptable.

"Okay. Then it's fine. So what tasks do I need to do?" I asked. Nikhil was watching me for long. He stood up from his chair and stepped towards balcony. I didn't want him to listen to my conversations so I asked him not to come and wait until I hung up the call. He was quite confused to see my gestures and later signalled me to throw the cigarette lighter. I did the needful. After getting the lighter he went back to work on his laptop.

"You may find these tasks quite twaddle. But if you truly need her then you will have to do it wholeheartedly," said Swati before explaining me the tasks. I was getting a bit scared from her words.

"What happened Aaryan? Are you there?" asked Swati after having no response from my end for a few moments.

"Sorry, I was just thinking something. I am ready to do it as long as it gets me closer to her," I said trying to sound quite confident.

"Okay. So here is your first task. Tomorrow morning, you need to collect fresh cow dung and place it at the entrance of your flat," said Swati. I was paralyzed to hear that.

"Are you serious? I mean, how keeping cow dung at the entrance is going to get me closer to her?" I asked for a clarification.

"I knew you would ask this. See Aaryan, I know it is quite tough. To be honest, if you can't do it then just finish all these discussions right now. I can't help you in that case. It is quite easy for someone to say he is in deep love, but it really requires guts to show and prove it. I don't think you have it," said Swati. She sounded quite rude. I decided, no matter what tasks she is going to put on me, no matter what would happen after 5 days, I would do the entire task and prove my love. At least one person in this world would realize that my love was true.

"Fine. I will do it," I said firmly. Honestly, I was still not ready. That moment I realized, heart and brain thinks differently. My heart said well done, whereas, the brain said, get lost.

"Great. So, tomorrow morning by 6:30 you need to complete this task. You may call me, if you need any guidance," said Swati. Meanwhile, Aarushi set her alarm for the said time so that they could make a call and confirm if I had done the task or not.

"But how will you know if I have done the task or not?" I asked.

"Nice question," said Swati and looked at Aarushi for an answer. Aarushi gestured her to ask for a selfie with the cow dung.

"I completely trust on you. I am sure you won't lie. But, I will appreciate if you can take a selfie of yours along with the cow dung," continued Swati.

"What the heck was that? She wanted me to take a shitty selfie! Who in this world has ever tried doing it?" I talked to myself. I was speechless and paralyzed. I couldn't even say no to her as she would again start doubting my true love and guts.

"Fine, if that is what makes you feel satisfied," I said annoyingly.

"Okay, then wish you all the best and talk to you tomorrow," said Swati after giving me the entire mental trauma.

"Yeah! Thanks. Good night!" I said and hung up the call.

It was 2:30 am and I just had another four hours to complete the task. Nikhil was slept, so I silently entered the room to make sure he doesn't wake up. I set the alarm for 5:00 am and lay down on the sofa. I was quite sure that I wouldn't get a sleep. Even if I had slept, I would have only dreamt of cows, shits and a shitty selfie.

Now there were two main challenges before me, firstly, where will I find cows in the morning and secondly, how will I make sure the dung is fresh.

Wait, there was one more challenge, and what will I explain to Nikhil? For me, the last challenge was the toughest one.

Chapter 9
First shitty selfie

* * *

It was still dark when the alarm started ringing. I got up and switched it off. Nikhil was in a deep sleep. I got up slowly and went to freshen up myself.

I was all set to make a move. Picked the bike's key and slowly opened the door. I locked the door from outside. Everything was quiet and calm until a stray dog, sleeping next to Nikhil's bike, woke up.

I ducked down, with a hope that he won't see me, but I was wrong. You can never cheat on a dog and a boss.

He turned his head, looked at me and then barked. I planned to walk slowly towards him.

Seeing me getting closer to him, he stood up and barked once more, but this time it was louder.

"Tommy, Tommy… keep quiet," I said. In India, most of the dogs, by default are named Tommy, similar to our Bollywood movies where most of the servants are either named *Ramu kaka* or *Chotu*.

The trick worked. Tommy waved his tail. I took out my pack of cigarettes, placed it in my mouth, and lured him until I dragged the bike outside the building campus. Tommy was following me with a hope of getting something to eat. I took out cigarettes from the pack and threw the empty packet at a distance. Tommy, like any other dog rushed to grab it.

I started the bike and drove as fast as I could. I felt sorry for Tommy as I made a fool out of him.

The weather was serene. I loved the quietness around.

It was tough to find a cow in the city, and even tougher to find cow dung. I needed someone's assistance to guide me. First, I thought of calling the lady astrologer, but later I dropped the plan as she might think I was dumb. So, I decided to ask a few oldies jogging on the roadside.

"Excuse me uncle," I said, stopping my bike. Uncle must have been in his fifties. He looked at me with shrunken eyebrows and took a step back.

"What do you want," he asked sceptically.

"Do you know if this area has a cow shelter?" I questioned him.

He smiled and asked if I wanted to buy milk.

"No uncle. I need some fresh cow dung," I replied giving race to my bike.

"Okay, so you need it for the house warming function," he replied. I thought to myself that how in a fraction of seconds can someone imagine things on his own without knowing the actual story. I then nodded in acceptance to his question as I didn't want him to throw another round of guess.

"Yes. I am surprised you guessed it so correctly," I smiled back at him.

He really felt proud of himself and said, "I have

not greyed my hair in Sun, and this is all because of my experience."

"Could you please tell me where can I find it?" I questioned him behind my fake smile.

"From the second signal, take left. Keep driving until you see a Krishna temple. There you will meet a priest named *Ghanshyam Ji.* He is the caretaker of that temple. He owns a cow too. You can ask him for the dung," he replied.

"Thank you so much for you help," I said and was about to leave when he stopped me and said, "In case you need sweets for the function, then here is my card. I am the owner of *Agra Sweets.*"

I was surprised to see that a businessman carries his visiting card even while jogging early morning. I took the card and left.

After a few minutes' drive, I reached the temple. The surroundings were quiet and the aroma of incense sticks was all around. Temple workers were busy cleaning the yard. I kept my slippers outside the entrance and went to offer my prayers to Lord Krishna.

"*Prabhu (Lord), I am not sure if I am doing something stupid or does it really makes some sense, but my love for her is pure. I won't lie to you as there is nothing hidden from you. I will do whatever it takes to make her realize my true feelings. Just make sure, when it happens, I am alive to listen those three beautiful words from her,*" I whispered in my prayer.

"It is for the first time that I am seeing a young man coming to the temple early morning," said a person wrapped in a saffron cloth. He was very fair. He wore Sandalwood beads around his neck and wore vermillion on his forehead.

I thought that he must be the priest that the uncle had referred to.

"Are you *Shri Ghanshyam Ji*?" I prefixed his name with Shri, because in India, it is a way to give respect.

"Yes," he said with a smile over his face. He was happy to hear his name.

"How do you know my name," he asked, as he doubted if he was that famous.

"An uncle told me about you," I replied.

"Who?" he questioned.

I was blank as I didn't know his name. But then I realized that I had his visiting card. I took it out and read his name.

"Agra sweets," I said as it was written in big bold letters.

"Oh, Gupta Ji," said the priest.

"Yes," I replied.

"Okay. So are you getting married?" asked the priest.

"What the hell?" I whispered. Now I knew why Mr Gupta and Sri Ghanshyam ji were good friends. Both of them were suffering from the same disease called, *pre-judge-mental-itis*.

"No," I said.

"Then why do you need a priest? Is there any function at your home?" another wild guess.

"No. I need a fresh cow dung cake," I said. My frustration level was at its extreme.

"Aah, now I got it. House warming function," he said happily and pulled my cheeks as if he had guessed it correctly. I gave up and agreed.

"You, too, guessed it correctly," I replied.

"I have not become a priest just like that, you see," he said proudly.

"Could I please get the dung?" I asked.

"Yes, yes sure. Come," he said and took me to the place where he kept his cow. A woman dressed in a blue saree was bathing the cow.

"Meet Kunti," said the priest.

"Namaste," I greeted the woman. She shrunken her eyebrows, gave a weird facial expression, and banged the bucket on the floor. After showing her angry face; she left the scene.

"Aah, she is not Kunti. She is Sheila. Kunti is the name of this holy mother cow," said the priest.

"Shit," I blabbered. "Did I just compare a woman with a cow," I asked myself and realized how double meaning it could have been.

"You can collect the dung from there. It is fresh," said the priest while feeding fodder to 'Ms Kunti'.

"Dude, seriously! Are you going to do this? Stop. This stinks," those ten seconds raised hundreds of questions in my mind. For a moment, I thought to step back, but then I realized that how important it was for me.

I bent down and collected the pile of fresh dung with both my hands and put it inside the plastic bag.

I was also happy from within that I was going to get Aarushi in my life soon..

"Thank you," I said with a smile to the priest. All my frustration had gone, and I was happy. I drove back to home.

This heavenly feeling didn't last for long as Tommy was standing right at the entrance, perhaps waiting for me. I could see anger on his face. I stopped my bike at the gate and looked at him. He stared at me and then he turned his face towards the plastic bag hanging on the bike's handle.

I knew, a few seconds more and he would jump to tear the plastic bag. I quickly took the bag and threatened him by pointing finger at him. He barked, just like any other cheated dog would do. I gathered some strength, parked the bike and ran up the stairs. Tommy barked for a while, but gave up soon.

It was 6:15 am. I was confident that Nikhil would have been slumbering. I took out the dung from the packet and put it near the entrance. Now, it was time to take a selfie.

I lay down on the floor and did the needful. I quickly opened my WhatsApp, and posted the image to the lady astrologer. It was so stupid of me for not asking her name.

Finally, I was done. I had completed the first chore. I felt as if I did everything to win Aarushi's trust and her love. And this tactile sensation was awesome, that if I was asked I would have even kissed the dung.

Now the problem was what would Nikhil say if he sees the dung at the entrance. I slowly unlocked the door and stepped inside like a stealer. Nikhil was still in his dreams and snoring loud. I too placed myself on the sofa for a quick snooze.

We woke up at 8 am and were ready within 30 minutes for office. The sad part was, that I had to bathe again in order to keep everything a secret. perform the nature call, bathe, and light touch once again to keep my stupidity a secret.

"Behen**** (fucker)," yelled Nikhil as he stepped over the dung. My eyes popped out as I was unsure how I was expected to act.

"Oh man. You just stepped over that shit," I laughed. With best friends, if you indicate your concern when they are screwed up, then you may fall under his suspicion.

"Who did this?" shouted Nikhil looking at his shoe, which was covered with the dung.

I walked near the door, faced at the dung for a while and said, "It looks like cow dung." But somehow it was not received well by Nikhil.

"You rascal, I will throw this on your face. I know this is cow dung, but who the hell has kept it here?" Nikhil said out of frustration.

"How would I know? I woke up with you. You should have checked before stepping out. Now give me the way," I said and skipped over the dung. Nikhil kept staring at his shoes and me. I maintained a secure distance from him as he could have got violent.

The whole journey from our home till office we had only one topic to discuss, "The mysterious cow dung."

He kept on blaming me for this, and I kept on lying.

That day at office, I kept looking at my WhatsApp for a message from the lady astrologer. Thanks to the technology, I knew that she had seen the picture I had sent.

"Aaryan, you got some time for me?" asked Mihir, my almost gay boss.

"Yep, sure," I said in acceptance.

He took me to his cabin and asked me to grab a chair.

"Look, I have to send someone to UK for a very important project. And it is going to be a long term project," explained Mihir in a very soft tone. For a software employee, onsite opportunity was like a blessing, which one could not afford to lose. I too got excited for a while.

"That's great. So what is going on in your mind?" I asked.

"I want you to go and take this task," he replied.

For a moment, I started imagining myself on London streets, roaming around with a beer in my hand and gazing at the white beauties walking on the bank of the Thames. But all of a sudden, Aarushi's face came before my eyes and the short and sweet London dreams, was over.

"Mihir thank you so much for this opportunity. I just wanted to know if I could borrow some time from you to get back on this," I asked him.

Mihir raised his eyebrows in shock and said,

"Sure, but I have never seen someone so thoughtful before accepting these kinds of opportunities. They all jump with joy"

"Even I am, but there are a few things that I need to settle down before I decide. I just need two days," I said.

Mihir nodded his head and wished me luck.

"You have got two days to decide. We have to have someone at the client's end by end of this month. So we need to hurry up," said Mihir, flipping pages of some file. I smiled and left his cabin.

'*Ting*', my mobile beeped. It was a message from the "Lady astrologer". That was the name I used while saving her number.

"*Great! You have passed your first task*," the message read.

"*Thanks. I want to talk to you urgently,*" I replied.

"*Regarding?????????*" I had no idea why she used so many question marks. Perhaps she was trying to showcase the gravity of her question.

"I can't type that much. Is it possible to talk now?" I asked her.

After waiting for almost 15 minutes, I got a reply, "*Ok*"

I quickly climbed up the stairs of my office terrace as it was the only quietest place to have private discussions.

"*Hello Aaryan.*"

"*Hi, hope you liked the shit selfie*," I said and as usual my joke was not received well.

"*What? What do you mean?*" she yelled.

"*Sorry, I mean, hope you appreciate my sincerity towards the task*," I covered up.

"*Yeah, absolutely. I am impressed. But, this is not what you wanted to discuss with me. You said, you have something important to share*," said the arrogant astrologer.

"I am getting an opportunity to visit UK for an onsite project," I told her.

"That's a great news! Congratulations!" she congratulated me out of excitement.

I was quite shocked as I didn't expect this reaction from an astrologer.

"Thanks, but I am quite worried," I expressed

"Why? What happened?" she asked.

"I am not sure what should I do? I mean, you have asked me to perform some tasks so that I can get Aarushi in my life and my boss has asked me to confirm within two days," I told her with a worried tone.

The lady astrologer could not speak for a while. She might have thought that their joke might cost me my career.

"Sorry. Is it okay if I call you after five minutes?" asked the astrologer.

"Why? What happened? Are you busy?" I felt she is going to leave my case as I was sounding selfish.

"No," she replied.

"No listen. I am ready to leave this opportunity as this may come any time in my life again, but Aarushi won't," I said with seriousness in my tone.

"No Aaryan. It's not like that. I understand you like Aarushi, but look at your age. You are a young man and getting this opportunity at the beginning of your career is a great thing. You should not miss this," she said politely.

"What? I didn't get it. Do you really think, stepping on a foreign land is more important than living in Aarushi's heart? I am sorry, but for me it's not that," I said.

"Are you sure?" she asked me.

"Woh aur honge jinhe saukh hai duniya bhatakne ka, Humme apne mehbbob ki nigahon mei, nazar-band hona hai" finally I expressed in the way I love the most.

"Okay, so you are a *shayar* too! Fine then, what do you expect from me?" she asked.

"Nothing. Actually before calling you I was quite confused, but now I know what I want. Thanks for picking up my call and talking to me. You have helped me in my decision," I said with confidence.

"Aaryan, listen. Please don't take any wrong step until you get my next message. Okay?" she told me.

"Okay. But I have already decided," I said and cut the call. I was happy, relaxed, and satisfied to the core of my heart. Perhaps that was the first time I realized it was love, not infatuation.

Chapter 10
Day-3

* * *

"Aaryan, wake up. You parents have come to meet you," said Ali Sir. He was hitting the bars with his black iron rod.

"Oh, what time is it?" I asked rubbing my eyes. It was quite cloudy. The sun was playing hide and seek with the clouds.

"It's 8 o'clock," said Ali Sir.

"I didn't realize that I have been sleeping until 8 am. Maybe it is because I had been writing the whole night.And how come noone wake me up?"

"Manoj told me that you were writing till 4 o'clock in the morning. So he didn't wake you up," said Ali pointing towards Manoj, the night patrol guard. Manoj looked at me and passed a smile. I too smiled back at him and said, "Manoj Sir, you can wake me up whenever you want to. Just two more days, and I will go to sleep mode, forever!"

I took a quick bath and did a quick prayer. Manoj

handcuffed me and escorted me to the visitor's area. I was excited to see my parents. My eyes were already filled with tears, but I tried to stay firm and calm.

I could see my parents from the passage. They were looking everywhere to have a glimpse of me. I entered the visitor's lobby. As per the law, the directives require a minimum of one staff person to escort the death row prisoner; hence Manoj came along with me.

"Aaryan beta," said my mom. I could see her happiness and helplessness. She wanted to touch me, wave my hair with love as she used to do when I was a child, but she couldn't as I was asked to sit quite far from the grilled window.

"How are you ma? I think you are not taking care of yourself. Papa, you had promised me that you would take care of her," I asked.

My mother looked so weak. Her eyes were shrunken; perhaps she had not slept for all these days.

"I am fine beta. You look so tired and weak. Aren't these men giving you food?" she said staring Manoj. I looked at Manoj and smiled.

"No ma. They all are very nice people. And I am getting proper food daily. You will never call me fat, and that's the problem with all mothers," I smiled.

"Beta, I have written a letter to the President. I am hoping that something good will happen," said my dad with hopes in his eyes.

"Papa, you need not worry so much. There is nothing you can do now. And moreover, I am a common man who has killed an MLA's only son. Who in our country is bothered to think about a common man's plea?" I said looking at my dad's eye.

"So what shall we do? Just wait for these guys to hang you and handover your dead body?" yelled my mom. She lost control over her tears and cried.

"Ma, please don't cry. That's my destiny, which I chose. And at least after my death you would be able to touch me and I would be sleeping on your lap," I said getting closer to the window. I wanted to wipe off her tears, but the handcuffs didn't allow me.

"Sir, is it possible that you let me hug my son?" said my dad. I had never seen him so deserted. I looked at Manoj for his decision. Bounded by the law; he nodded his head to express his limitations. I knew he was not wrong as he was just doing his duty.

"Papa, why are you so worried? You are our family's hero. Please don't do this. I may not be able to stop my tears for long," I requested my dad. He wiped his tears and stood firm.

"How is Aarushi?" I asked. My parents looked at each other and were perhaps trying to frame a pleasant answer for my question.

"Please say the truth," I interrupted them

"She is still in coma. Nikhil is there with her," said Papa. I could not say anything, but closed my eyes to stop my tears from revealing.

"I don't know what are you trying to achieve? You have not spoken a single word in your defense," pleaded mom.

"When they were cruel and destroyed my life, everyone in the city was blind. I was the only witness of the crime that was planned against me. Who was going to believe me, a common man?" I said. My mom turned her face away and wiped her tears.

"Aaryan, now it's time to move," said Manoj showing me the big round wall clock. My parents couldn't restrict themselves from pleading Manoj and requested him for a few more minutes. My mom was trying to pass her fingers from the grill of the window so that she could at least touch me. I went closer to her and touched her fingers and then even I

could not cease myself from shedding tears.

I took their blessings and left. Manoj was feeling bad, but he explained his limitations.

"No problem Sir, I completely understand it," I said while Manoj was locking me inside the cell.

"I don't know what the truth is, but I am sure; you can't be a murderer. Look at yourself; a learned, disciplined, polite person like you must have gone through a huge trauma to commit this crime," said Manoj.

I smiled and said, "Uske khoon ka ilzaam bhi humare sar par hai, jisne humme har roz zehar pilaya."

Chapter 11
You are an idiot

* * *

"Aarushi, try to understand. He is getting an onsite opportunity. It's about his career," said Swati. Aarushi kept her eyes glued to the book called, "India after Gandhi". Though I do have respect for the father of the nation, but honestly I didn't like his interference in my spoiled love life.

"Am I really stopping him from going? Ask him to go. I will feel blessed if he goes. At least you will get time to prepare for your exams. I am anyway, out of this stupidity," explained Aarushi while writing notes.

"You are not stopping him. But he is stopping himself. And there is no harm if you meet him once and say no. I promise you, it will get over," explained Swati annoyingly.

"Are you sure, he will leave me?" asked Aarushi closing the book. Swati, though was doubtful as she knew that it was not easy considering my madness, she instead nodded her head in assurance.

"Fine, then ask him to meet me tomorrow at the Starbucks in Sector-18," said Aarushi passing a cunning smile. She was all set to say no.

"I don't know about your priorities, but I feel it's never wrong to have someone in your life who loves you and respects you," said Swati and took out her phone to message me.

My phone beeped and I saw a message from the lady astrologer. The message read: "Hi, the astrology ball shows that you will meet her tomorrow at the Starbucks in Sector-18."

Nikhil and I were having tea at Salim's shop. Nikhil was still under the mental trauma of the shit he stepped onto. Salim was the eleventh person to whom Nikhil was sharing his grievance. A few people related this to evil practices performed by witches. And some overly genius species left on earth said, "Mother cow must have came to your home to give you blessings."

But honestly, the best comment was from Salim.

"*Bhaiya, jo chiz aapke dimaag mei hoti hai, wohi chiz aapko dikhti hai.*" *(Brother, you see what is there in your mind)* "Who knows, someone might have kept a black forest cake, and you felt it was a cow dung cake," said Salim while tuning his old radio.

I was laughing. More than Salim's comment, what annoyed Nikhil most was my laugh.

"Stupid, *jyada mat bol.* I will bring that black forest cake and paste it on your face," said Nikhil while warning Salim.

"*I can see that, you will meet her tomorrow!*" popped another message from the lady astrologer.

My heart beat faster and my brain started framing the conversation, which might take place in the evening.

"*Are you sure? Where, when, how? I am really*

excited!" I replied.

"*You will meet her at Starbucks in Sector-18 at 6:30 pm tomorrow,*" read the message.

"Man, either she is making me fool or she is really a great astrologer," I thought to myself, reading the details mentioned in the message. Though, I had a doubt, but I wanted to give it a try.

"Either, I will meet Aarushi today or I will leave the lady astrologer," I decided.

"*But how would Aarushi know that she is going to meet me at Starbucks?*" I messaged her back and cleared my genuine doubt.

"*I am controlling her fate too. Don't you dare ask me these questions again. I am an astrologer and I can see future. Next time if you doubt me, I will leave,*" threatened Swati, the arrogant astrologer.

"Okay, chill, I won't doubt you," I replied her. I had no other option other than agreeing to what she said.

Swati showed my last message to Aarushi. Aarushi smiled and took the phone from Swati.

"*You will meet her, but you will never ever get her,*" texted Aarushi from Swati's mobile. Swati didn't like Aarushi's ruthless behaviour. She took her mobile and switched it off as she knew, once the message gets delivered to me, I was going to destroy her peace.

Meanwhile, Nikhil and I had reached our flat, after finishing the 'shit' talk and the awesome tea. Nikhil, as usual, grabbed a beer bottle and sat in front of his computer. He looked puzzled for a while, and then opened Google to search "Cow shit at door means". I controlled my laugh and came out of the room.

I took my mobile out and read the message.

"What the hell?" I got furious and called the

astrologer. But her mobile was switched off. It frustrated me even further. Finally, I took out my nicotine sticks and smoked out my anger.

Chapter 12
Starbucks

* * *

"Hey, where are you?" asked Nikhil over the phone

"I am driving. I will call you later," I said.

"Driving? You rascal, you went out without even telling me," yelled Nikhil.

I had taken his bike whilst he was sleeping. If I had told him, I knew, he would have bombarded endless questions.

"Bhai, I will come at night. Don't worry," I said and hung up the call.

"Go to hell. Don't call me ever again," he messaged me to show his anger. I smiled and ignored.

I reached Starbucks and parked my bike at its basement. I thought of waiting for Aarushi outside and go to the coffee shop together once she comes.

"I started smoking while waiting for her. I took just one puff, when a constable from the traffic police's tow truck jumped before me.

"Who's scooty is this?" he asked me. He looked quite young and was dressed in a yellow color t-shirt and green trousers. I smiled back at him.

"I am asking you a question?" he raised his voice. There was a grey colour scooty, which was parked at the no parking zone. I thought lets have some more fun before the date, so I lied to him.

"Okay, let me check. Its TVS scooty," I said with a big smile on my face. Trust me, my smile was so impactful that the constable lost his patience and approached towards the Scooty.

"You think we are jokers? You are standing next to it, that means it' s yours," he exclaimed.

"Yes, it's mine," I said firmly.

"Move it from here or else we will tow it," he threatened.

"Tow it," I said exhaling the smoke out of my chest. This made the other two persons sitting inside the truck furious. They came out of the truck, blabbered a few slangs to show their anger and picked the Scooty and placed it in the truck.

"Now come and collect it from the police station," said the driver and they left. I waved my hands and said 'bye, bye'!

"How is your date going?" messaged the lady astrologer. At first I decided to call her and ask her that why did she say that I would never get Aarushi in my life, but I didn't want to spoil my mood, so I messaged her.

"I am waiting for her. She is yet to come," he messaged.

"She is sitting there waiting for you," messaged Swati. After reading that message, I relay wanted to wash the feet of that 'someone' who has always said that 'When you fall in love, you get mad'. I never realized that how did the lady astrologer know the details in depth.

I read the message and ran as fast as I could. Two stairs at a time. I could hear my heart beat, which was thumping fast.

There she was, the most beautiful girl I have ever seen. She wore a yellow salwar suit accompanied by a white dupatta. Her hair was a rich shade of mahogany. It flowed in waves to adorn her glowing, porcelain-like skin. Her eyes, framed by long lashes, were bright, and seemed to brighten the world. A straight nose, kissable cherry lips, she seemed the picture of perfection.

"What should I say? Or should I just wait for her to look at me or I just go and sit beside her," all these questions had occupied my tiny brain.

"Yes Sir, how may I help you?" asked an employee of the Starbucks, who was dressed in a black attire.

"I am with her," I said pointing towards Aarushi. My voice was loud enough to get Aarushi's attention. She looked at me and smiled to confirm, I was with her.

"It's the time. Now or never. Give your best. Dear God, be with me," I prayed and pulled the chair to sit. Still nervous, I preferred to keep quiet until she begins.

"Hi," she said with a cute little smile on her face. But that smile was enough to move me into a paralytic state.

"Shall we order something?" she asked tucking the strands of hair behind her ears. I was still numb. Eyes denied to blink and lips denied to open themselves.

"Look, they won't allow us to sit idle without ordering anything from the menu. So, if you can talk then it would be really helpful," whispered Aarushi moving a little closer to the table.

"Yeah, why not. Let's order something," I said and picked the menu card placed on the table. Trust me, I behaved like a moron.

"What would you like to have," I asked her.

"A Java Chip Frappuccino for me," she said in a single breath. God, how do girls pronounce these tough tongue twister menu items so easily? If I had to order this, I would have preferred calling the waiter and pointing my choice on the menu card.

"Could you please repeat? I just heard JAVA," I sounded confused. She smiled and moved her hand forward.

"God, she wants to shake hand with me," my brain cells were jumping in joy. I got a huge smile on my face. I too brought my hand forward and held hers. Her palm was warm and soft like silk. It felt like electricity passed through my body.

"Hello, I need the menu card not a handshake," she said pulling her hands back.

"Oh, sorry. I thought, you wanted to do a handshake," I said passing the menu card to her. She took the menu card, and gave a suspicious gesture to me.

"I have decided what I need. Let's go to the counter and order," she said and stood. I too joined her.

"One Java Chip Frappuccino for me and..." she looked at me for my choice of coffee.

"*Same to same kar do ji* (same coffee for me too)," I said with a confident smile on my face.

"Okay, ma'am. Two java chip frappuccino. Would you like to have anything else," asked the girl behind the counter. She looked at me with a smile; perhaps she had judged that I was a dumb fellow. Stupid girl!

"Naah... that's it," said Aarushi and we got back to our place. "I love Java chip. You know why, because I am JAVA developer, and I love JAVA," I started talking non-sense. Aarushi was listening to me patiently with a soothing smile on her face.

"My favorite cricketer is 'JAVAgal Srinath', favorite

song is Mar JAVA, mit JAVA," I kept talking until Aarushi broke into a laugh. That was the best moment in my life.

"You are funny. But let me tell you one thing, you have made a girl wait for you, and that is not a good thing," she said shrinking her eyebrows to show her anger.

"No, I was not late. In-fact I was standing downstairs waiting for you. Then I received a message from my astrologer, who said that you were already here," I vomited my secret. An idiotic secret.

"An astrologer?" asked Aarushi. Though she knew to whom I was referring to as an astrologer, but she behaved to be unaware of the whole thing. I didn't know how to fix my screwed situation, so I decided to change the topic.

"Hell with that astrologer. You know, while I was waiting for you," I tried to change the topic. Though the "Hell" word didn't go well with the beautiful lady, but I was hardly bothered about it at that moment.

"A tow truck came. I was sitting over a scooty and was smoking," I again screwed myself. Another word "Smoking" was added as an ingredient to destroy the peace on Aarushi's face. I thought if I gave her a chance to speak, she would definitely kick my balls, so I continued.

"Those traffic persons thought I was the owner of that scooty and asked me to park it at the proper parking place. I denied and said, I won't park it, do whatever you can," I tried to sound like a cool dude, but was failing badly and gradually.

"You know what happened then?" I asked to check if Aarushi was still listening to me or not. Aarushi gestured me to continue.

"They picked the scooty and dumped it on their truck and left," I said and laughed. "It was so funny, you know," I said smiling and hoping Aarushi too would pass a smile, at least a fake one.

"Was it a grey colour scooty?" asked Aarushi looking tensed.

"Yeah. You too noticed that? Don't know who that idiot was," I smiled and took the glass of water to take a sip.

"That was my scooty," said Aarushi looking straight into my eyes. I choked and my eyes popped out. I had no clue if it was going to be the best day or the worst day of my life.

"Fuck" I said. She stood and asked me to come along with her.

"Where are we going?" I asked while we were leaving the Starbucks. She remained silent and kept walking. I knew the volcano was all set to erupt as soon as we reached downstairs.

"Ma'am, your order is ready," said the girl who took our coffee order. I looked at the girl and then looked at Aarushi. Aarushi too looked at the girl and then looked at me. Now, it was the girl's chance to look at both of us, and she did. I knew what I had to do. I took 1,000 rupees out of my wallet and paid the bill.

"Sorry, it's an emergency," I said and ran as Aarushi had already left.

"I am really sorry, I never meant to say you're an idiot," I said while trying to match Aarushi's speed.

"Do you really think, it's the idiot word for which I am worried?" Aarushi stopped and turned to yell at me.

"Then was it that f-word?" I asked. Her face turned red with anger and she shouted, "You idiot, that was my scooty. And because of you, now I am in trouble," yelled Aarushi. I looked around to check who else saw me getting scolded by a beautiful girl. Luckily, there was no one other than a street dog, who stopped to listen to the argument.

"Now it's your responsibility to get my scooty back," warned Aarushi. I nodded my head in acceptance as I hardly had any choice.

"Okay, I will get my bike and then let's go to the police station," I said trying to calm her down. She was busy typing something on her mobile.

"Are you updating your Facebook status, like, feeling sad about my cute scooty with Aaryan Rathod and a street dog," I said with an intention to bring a smile on her face, but I failed badly. I left the scene to bring my bike from the parking.

"Are you nuts? If you don't get the scooty back, you will never get Aarushi in your life," a text message from the lady astrologer beeped on my mobile.

"How did she know about this incident? Is she following me, or is she really so powerful," I was shocked.

"How do you know about this incident? And please don't use these if-else conditions with me. It's my love story and not a fucking programming language," I texted her back.

Never had I thought that my first date would be so adventurous. We didn't even talk a single word to understand each other. All we talked was that Java chip Frappuccino, the coffee that could not even reach our taste buds.

"Let's go," I said giving race to my bike. Aarushi sat on the pillion seat.

"Okay, so just to be on the safer side, let me clarify something," I said looking at Aarushi through the side mirror. She looked at me with frustration.

"See there may be some speed breakers and lots of traffic, so I need to use breaks and sometimes sudden brakes," I continued.

"So, please hold the side bar or else you may think, I am just applying brakes for wrong intentions," I said.

"Just shut up and drive," ordered Aarushi.

After 20 minutes of driving, jumping three speed breakers and applying brakes almost more than 14 times, we reached the police station. And during this, I was able to get Aarushi lean on my back twice. It was an amazing feeling. Though Aarushi warned me not to repeat this again, but I was feeling rewarded and blessed the guy who made those speed breakers.

"Look that is my scooty," said Aarushi and ran towards the scooty parked at the station. She was inspecting each and every corner of the scooty to make sure it wasn't damaged.

"Hello Madam, is this your scooty," asked a policeman

"Yes it is," replied Aarushi, still inspecting.

"Shall we take it," I asked the policeman. He looked at me and asked who I was.

"I am her boyfriend," I replied with a big smile. The policeman looked at me with suspicious eyes. And to supplement his suspicion, Aarushi too made a shocked face.

"Oh, so you came to take your scooty," I heard someone shouting from my back. To my shock, he was the same constable whom I had shown my cool attitude a few hours' back.

"Sir, actually, I had a fight with my girlfriend, so I was behaved rudely with you. I am sorry sir," I apologised.

"Aaryan, come here," gestured Aarushi. She could not digest the word "girlfriend".

"When did I become your girlfriend? Don't even dream of it," warned Aarushi. She didn't raise her voice else I would have been in jail for eve-teasing.

"You need to pay fine," said the policeman adjusting the frequency of his walky-talky.

"How much?" asked Aarushi. The tow man and the policeman looked at each other to decide the amount.

"Sir, you must have some standard fine for these issues. What is that?" I asked, as I was quite sure they were going to loot us.

"Don't teach us our standards. We know what is your standard. You fight with your girlfriend and get her scooty towed," said the constable angrily. I didn't feel bad as there was at least one more person who referred Aarushi as my girlfriend. Aarushi again got impatient listening to that word.

"Tell us the amount. I need to go," said Aarushi looking at me with anger.

"What, I didn't say this time. He said it," I whispered in my defense.

"Rs 5,000," said the policeman. He almost gave a minor heart attack to us. Before we could have given a counter offer, a guy interrupted us.

"Are you asking for a fine or buying the girl," said the guy taking a cigarette out of his jeans. He was almost 6ft tall, bearded, dark complexion. He wore a black kurta over a pair of jeans. There were two guys accompanying him as assistant. The policeman, took out a matchbox from his pocket and helped the guy lit his cigarette. I felt like kicking him between his legs.

"*Kya bola be*? (What did you say?)" I approached the rascal folding my sleeves. Yes, he was a rascal, and I didn't find some less offensive synonym to describe him. The other two guys, who were standing beside him, came forward to stop me.

"*Oye, hero mat ban* (Don't try be a hero). You don't know him. He is Himanshu Joshi, son of our MLA, Dayal Joshi," said the policeman pulling me aside.

"So does it mean he can say anything to a girl. And moreover, you are a policeman, aren't you here to do your duty for a common man? Or are you just a puppet of these spoiled brats," I said to the policeman angrily.

"Listen, if I wish, I can kill you right now. Take this

girl, rape her, and throw her at some street, But today is my birthday, and I am not in a mood to do this. So it would be better if you just leave," said Himanshu, gripping my collar and exhaling the smoke on my face.

I wished for a second that had I been alone that day, I bet, I would have reduced the count of rascals on this planet by one.

"Aaryan, please stop this now. Let's go," said Aarushi, handing Rs5,000 to the policeman. She looked tensed. I could see tears in her eyes. I was feeling restless. My heart knows how badly I wanted to hit that bastard.

"I am leaving, but trust me I will not die unless I kill you. Mark my words, you will not be alive to celebrate your next birthday," I said pointing finger at that bastard.

"Before you kill him, I think I need to answer him," said Aarushi and came forward. In the next second, a tight slap was registered on Himanshu's cheek. Everyone was stunned. A girl slapped an MLA's son on his birthday.

"Dare not to say this for a girl again. If you are really desperate to rape a girl, start from your own family," said Aarushi and asked me to start the bike.

"Leave them. Now you just count days. Both of you. I am going to make your life hell, I promise," said Himanshu stopping his assistants, who were trying to get hold of us.

Aarushi and I started our bike and left. The whole way, I was just thinking, about Aarushi. I needed to talk to her. I didn't want her to go back to her room, depressed.

Before I could have approached her to stop driving, she herself slowed down and gestured me to park the bike at the side of the road. We stopped our bike near a tea shop.

"I would like to have a cup of tea," said Aarushi placing her helmet on the seat. Her eyes were blood red.

"Sure, I will get it," I said and asked the tea vendor for two cups of tea. I was just worried, how would I bring her back to normal. This was our first serious meet, which I considered as a date and it was all screwed.

I took the tea glasses, walked towards her and said, "Your Java chip frappuccino, madam," I was standing like a robot, damn serious, no expression.

She looked at me for a while and then started laughing. She laughed until she got tears in her eyes. I was so relaxed to see her normal. I too got my smile back.

"Why did you say him that, you would kill him before you die?" asked Aarushi taking a sip.

"I don't know. I just said it. If I had a gun with me, I would have even fulfilled my promise then and there. And moreover, it was not a promise made to him but to you," I said looking at Aarushi's eye.

"I want to get rid of my tension," said Aarushi.

"Me too," I supported her. "What do you generally do when you are tensed or sad?" asked Aarushi taking a sip.

"Drink" I replied, honestly. Even if I would have lied, she could have easily caught me.

"And let me guess, you would be doing the same thing, even when you are happy, right?" said Aarushi sarcastically and smiled.

"Yeah, right. That is the best medicine to forget pain and celebrate happiness," I said proudly as if it was a very good habit.

"You know, I don't drink neither I have ever entered a bar or a club," said Aarushi making puppy eyes. God promise, she looked so cute that I wanted to seal my lips with hers. Definitely some supernatural forces stopped me to do so.

"Hmm, what can I say," I sighed as I had no answer for that, and was not even sure, whether that was an indirect question.

"Will you take me to a club today? I want to try

how alcohol tastes," she said looking at me for an answer.

I was at cloud nine. But then I became quite cautious. Is it a test to check if I take girls to club? Is she trying to test my character? Is the date still on, which I thought was over when we stepped out of the Starbucks? and many more questions started making rounds in my brain.

"Hello? Are you listening?" said Aarushi waving her hand

"Yeah of course. Why not? That would be fun," I said, still nervous. We planned to keep our bikes at our room and go by cab.

"Drinking and driving" is a punishable offence, and honestly we already had a bad day.

We reached at our place, my room and her hostel.

"Okay, so, see you in 5 minutes," I said.

"5 minutes! Are you kidding me? I need at least 15 minutes to get ready," she said.

"Fine, then, 15 minutes, and we meet downstairs," I said and we left to our respective rooms.

"*Sale harami aagaya tu* (You bastard)," said Nikhil as soon as I entered the room.

"Bhai, I went for a date," I said throwing his bike key on the sofa. Nikhil looked at me and was about to say something before I interrupted him.

"Technically, I am still in a date. Because now in another 15 minutes, we will be going to a club," I said to Nikhil holding his arms.

"We? You mean, me and you?" asked Nikhil with a hopeful smile on his face.

"Shut up you stupid. I am going with Aarushi," I said with a proud smile covering my face.

"What the ****? Seriously? How did you do it bro!" jumped Nikhil with joy.

That's an advantage of having best friends. They

feel happy when you are happy and they feel happier when you are screwed, as they know you are never alone.

"It's a long story and I will tell you once I am back. I will get fresh now, got just 10 minutes more," I said and went to the washroom.

I was about to lock the door when Nikhil jumped in, "Bhai, would you mind, if I come at the balcony to see you guys," said Nikhil holding the door.

"Dekh lena sale, but please book a cab for us," I ordered.

"Okay done," said Nikhil and took his mobile out to book the cab. Meanwhile, I took a bath and dressed myself for the party.

"*Bhai kaisa lag raha hu (*Bro, how do I look?)," I asked Nikhil. I was dressed in a black shirt and a grey trouser. I believe, I looked handsome.

"*Maa* kasam (Swear on my mom), if I would have been a gay, I would have proposed you right now," said Nikhil kissing me on my cheek. I pushed him aside and gave him some classic slang.

"Hey, the cab has arrived," said Nikhil. He went to the balcony and gestured me to go downstairs and wished me luck. He was standing at the balcony waiting for us to board the cab. I knew he just wanted to have a glimpse of Aarushi.

I went downstairs and was waiting for Aarushi to come. "Wait, where the hell are we going," I asked myself and looked at Nikhil who was bending himself from the balcony grill to look for Aarushi.

"Bhai, which club are you sending us?" I asked Nikhil as he had only booked the cab.

"Quantum Club, Sector-18," yelled Nikhil. "And don't forget to try the Champagne cocktail, it's amazing," suggested the alcoholic king.

"Oh Man!" said Nikhil. His mouth was wide open and eyes popped out. I looked back, and there she was.

Dressed in a white dress with a golden belt around the waist, she was looking no less than an angel. She turned towards me. Few strands of hair obstructed her face. She tucked them behind her ears. She wore a nice dangler in her ears. Her eyes were twinkling. Her pure white face gave one an illusion that it would turn red if anyone touched her. No straight guy could ever take his eyes off her golden nose-ring. Her lips, pure pink, never needed any extra colour. So lively, so perfect, mesmerizing, alluring, delighting, enthralling… I never found enough words to describe her.

I was scared to face her. I thought, I looked enough handsome to qualify for a date with her, but I was losing my confidence. I decided to hide behind the cab. She saw me and sighed.

A chill ran down my body. I was unable to move. I choked. My hands curled. I managed to walk towards her, whilst my eyes were still locked to hers.

"Dhadkan ko thaame rakhna, aaj mushkil ho raha hai Jhuki hai jo teri palki, dil bekaabu ho raha hai"

"What did you blabber?" asked Aarushi. She noticed me reciting the shayari.

"Aah, nothing. You are looking amazingly beautiful in this dress," I said appreciating her looks. She smiled adjusting her watch.

"You should at least say something about me," I asked raising my hand in air like Bollywood superstar Shahrukh Khan. She laughed and said, "Shall we start, because your friend standing at the balcony is going to fall soon. She pointed at the balcony from where Nikhil was leanaing on the railing. He stood there as an idiot and kept laughing.

I opened the door for Aarushi, which I hope she

appreciated, and she got inside.

"Do you want me to sit at the front, or is it okay if I sit at rear along with you?" I asked with a smile on my face. She looked at me, smiled and then picked her red colored leather purse, which she had earlier kept on the middle seat, and placed it on her lap.

"I take this as yes," I said and got inside the cab. No idea, what to do next. I had seen actors in Hollywood movies, kissing their date. Honestly, I too wanted to seal those beautiful lips with mine, but I knew, another one inch towards her, and I end up getting a tight slap on my cheek. So, I killed my idea.

"I am starting the meter," said the chauffeur. He was a young man, well dressed and behaved professionally as he didn't adjust his mirror to have a glimpse of Aarushi.

"Sure, let's go," I said adjusting my trousers.

I didn't know how to start the conversation. I looked at Aarushi, and smiled, hoping that she would initiate. She too smiled back and then started looking outside the window. Perhaps, this time she wanted me to initiate.

"Shall I ask you something?" I said in a very soft tone, as I didn't want the chauffeur to hear our conversation.

"Yep" she replied. Her eyes were so expressive, that one could easily get hypnotized, just by a glance. I tried to control myself.

"Aren't you afraid of going out with me? I mean, you know me, you have seen me doing idiotic things. There was a time when I destroyed your peace and you hated me so much," I said, avoiding eye contact. I lacked guts to look at her and speak. This is the problem with the genes of bachelors in India. We are masters of eve teasing, writing love letters and doing all sorts of non-sense things, but when it comes to face-to-face interaction with our loved ones, our tongue and the vocal chords go on a silent mode. We are only left with a slow-functioning brain.

"Look here," she said. I turned towards her.

"Until yesterday, I was, but after having the Java chip Frappuccino with you, I am not," said Aarushi in a heart pleasing tone, looking straight into my eyes. I swear I fell in love with her a million times within those few seconds. I smiled. Actually sighed.

"But, we didn't have that coffee," I said sadly.

"No we had it right. Don't you remember the roadside StarSucks tea stall," she taunted and smiled. I was falling in love with her every moment. I wished the cab driver kept driving the whole night. I wished that the journey doesn't end..

"There is one thing more that I wanted to ask. Actually, I am quite curious to know, why did you slap that guy? I mean, no doubt, he deserved it, but how did you do it? Generally, I have not seen girls being so brave in these scenarios. I must say, it was really amazing to watch you do it," I asked, this time I had my eyes locked with hers. I was feeling confident now.

"You know when we decided to leave from the police station, I thought how am I going to justify this day to myself once I become an IAS officer. How will I make sure that women in the city are safe if I don't have enough guts to fight against these insecurities? So, I thought to teach him a lesson and I went ahead to slap him. Was it too hard?" asked Aarushi making an innocent face. I nodded my head to say, no.

"It was a good one. Right on the spot," I replied giving her thumbs up. I heard an ambulance alarm. It was struggling to find a space in the traffic. An usual scene in our country, where traffic is cleared for politicians and not for the ambulance.

"*Bhaiya*, please get the cab aside and give a way for

the ambulance," I requested the driver. He nodded his head and steered the cab to the left. Ambulance passed by us, and for a moment I closed my eyes and prayed for the one inside fighting for his life.

Aarushi noticed me doing the prayer and she could not restrict herself to ask, "Do you pray whenever you see an ambulance?"

I was quite surprised and felt sighed that she noticed my secret prayer. I nodded to say, yes. She smiled and said, "Good."

"Would you mind if I ask something personal?" she asked.

"No. We are on our first date, and we must utilize this time to know each other," I said. Though, the "date" did raise Aarushi's eyebrows, but she digested it.

"So is our date still on?" asked Aarushi with a cunning smile on her face.

"Yes. Do you doubt?" I said smiling. She smiled back to accept my hypothesis.

"Okay, so did you have someone, very closer to you, whom you carried in an ambulance and that is the reason, you understand the pain one goes through and so you offer your prayers for them," asked Aarushi.

"Never and I really wish that it never happens to anyone. You know, that is the time, when a person or a family needs God to help them out. I just act as another person on earth who tries to plead the God on their behalf," I explained.

"You are not that bad," said Aarushi, punching on my arms. I was on cloud nine, just by her touch.

After a few more smiles-talks and chance to admire her beauty we reached our destination.

"*Bhaiya*, we have reached," said the driver closing the meter.

"Let's share the bill," said Aarushi, accessing her wallet.

"No please. I know you are an independent girl, but already because of me, you had to pay Rs 5,000. So, let me take care of this," I said and paid the bill.

"Quantum Club" said Aarushi reading the fancy board at the entrance of the club.

"Is it the place where you come often?" asked Aarushi adjusting her dress.

"Nope. This is the first time. This was Nikhil's choice. If you don't like it then I will bring Nikhil to you and you can poison him to death," I said to which she laughed.

The place was quite dark, and we could hear the music blaring as we stood in line. It was crowded and people were pushing each other to get a quick entry inside the club. Bouncers standing at the entrance were having a tough time managing the crowd.

I was quite cautious for Aarushi. This was her first time, and I didn't want any bad experience for her. Already we had one. I was covering Aarushi from both the sides so that no one could push her. She looked back at me and smiled. I behaved responsibly.

After having a quick look at our IDs, the bouncer placed a stamp, which read "QC" on our forearms.

There were multi-colored flash lights on the dance floor, but they were not bright enough to reach beyond that. It was very crowded. As I assisted our way to the bar, people dancing rubbed up against me. Finally we found our way to an empty barstool at a corner.

"God, this is madness," said Aarushi, finally taking a breath of relief. I could not have agreed more.

By now, our eyes were adjusting to the imminent darkness. Bright spots of neon beer signs on the wall stood out, illuminating the faces and cleavage of the crowd, while others disappeared into the contrasting blackness.

"What are they doing?" asked Aarushi gesturing me to look at the table behind me. I slowly turned back to have a glance. A guy and girl were engrossed in a lip lock position. They were trying to invade inside each other with their tongue. I was really enjoying the scene, as it is quite rare in our country, where you can piss in public, but can't kiss.

"I think they are on their first date. It is a holy practice that one has to perform on their first date," I said sarcastically, to which Aarushi made a shocked face.

"Don't even think of it," said Aarushi gesturing a slap to me. I giggled.

"So, I will get you a breezer and anything you would like to have for snacks," I asked for her choice.

"What is breezer?" asked Aarushi curiously. I was looking around to check if anyone was having it so that I could show her, when Aarushi fired another question.

"Shall we go at the bar and decide?" asked Aarushi. She was curious to see the list of drinks, which was offered. I could not deny and we went to the bar.

"See, you are a beginner and I would suggest you to start with a breezer," I said pointing her to the cranberry breezer kept on the shelf along with several others.

"What would you take?" she asked scanning all the bottles kept on the shelf.

"I would go for a scotch," I said, listening to which she made some confused face and then she started waving her hand to get the bartender's attention. It was quite funny as she was saying, "*Bhaiya humme bhi pila do* (brother, give us some drink too)".

"Yes, beautiful lady, what would you like to have?" asked the bartender whilst busy in making some cocktail. He was juggling the bottles, and was doing all sort of creativities required to be the best in this field.

"Two glasses of scotch," replied Aarushi. She literally had to shout so that bartender could hear her.

"Scotch? Are you sure? You won't like its taste, trust me," I tried to convince her, but failed. She asked me to stand behind her while she places the order.

"Which one," asked the bartender pointing towards the several scotches kept on the shelf. Aarushi pinched my stomach for the answer.

"Ouch, … Black dog," I whispered in pain.

"Is it a drink? Or you are trying to make fun of me?" Aarushi turned to confirm.

"It is a drink, look there," I answered pointing her towards the Black dog bottle kept on the shelf.

"Black dog," replied Aarushi. The bartender could not listen as the music was too loud and he was occupied with other orders.

"*Bhaiya*, Black dog dedo (Brother, give us Black dog)," yelled Aarushi, and he nodded and melted away into the cries of a hundred other thirsty patrons.

The guy with the pony tail, finally found a time for us and in a moment later, before Aarushi's thought was even finished, her two pegs of scotch slid in front of her, and the bartender was gone before she could even look up to mouth the words "Thanks".

We took our glasses and went back to our table. With God's grace, it was not occupied.

"Aah, that was interesting," she said relaxing her shoulders. Her fair skin was glowing even in the dark ambience. I was getting high just by looking at her.

"Shall we do cheers now?" she asked raising the glass. I too raised mine and did the cheers, "To the first date!" I said to which she just answered with her killing smile.

She took her first sip. Her facial expression kept

changing with the spirit making its way through her throat. She forcibly closed her eyes and said, "Yuck."

"How do you guys drink this? It doesn't taste sweet," she said keeping her glass on the table.

"This is the problem when you drink for the first time. And that's the reason I wanted to you to start with a breezer, which you would have found sweeter than this," I replied taking another sip.

"No it's okay. I can handle it," she said and took another sip. I loved the faces she was making with every sip. Just like other first timers, she too finished her first peg in less than 5 minutes. I was still left with mine.

"You drink slow man, I thought you were a drunkard," she said. I could notice that it was the alcohol and the music which was getting high on her. I just smiled and tried not to answer her.

"Aaryan, there is a very beautiful girl behind you. You can't afford to miss her," she said and gestured me to look behind.

"Is she more beautiful than you," I asked trying to complete my peg.

"I don't know. May be yes," she said raising her shoulders and eyebrows simultaneously.

I did the bottoms up, hit the glass on the table and said, "What if I turn back, and she looks at me and then in a matter of second we fall in love with each other."

Aarushi laughed madly and said, "I never knew that a glass of peg could actually make a guy overconfident."

"Okay, in that case, let me have my chance on her," I said and turned to look for the girl we were talking about. Aarushi stood beside me to hunt for her. "There she is. Red dress, high heels," she said. She was dancing on the floor with her friends. She looked hot, but not beautiful.

"What did you like in her," asked Aarushi. We both

were looking at the girl and talking.

"Her figure," the alcohol in me spoke.

"What? You guys are the same. You just look at figures," she was frustrated and angry on me.

"What did you want me to notice in her? I am also a guy and moreover I am drunk right now," I said in my defense.

"Okay, what was the first thing you noticed when you saw me?" asked Aarushi tucking her hair behind her ears to give me a clear access to her amazingly crafted face. I was smiling.

"Why are you smiling?"

"This is the first time, you are asking me to look at you closely. Isn't it great" I said with a huge smile on my face.

"Please. I have asked you a question. What did you notice first when you saw me," she reiterated her question. I got serious this time.

"Dare not look below my chin," she warned placing her index finger on her chin to clarify the premises I was allowed to look into.

"Shall I answer it later? I mean, I would like to go for the next round," I said making an innocent face and showing her my empty glass. She nodded in agreement and we went to repeat our order.

"And one thing more. Promise me that you won't use my answer as a weapon to disqualify me as your lover," I said while Aarushi was counting the number of ice in her peg. She looked at me with least interest and then resumed her counting.

We were now 3 pegs down. Fortunately, we found ourselves a place to sit and talk. Aarushi was totally high and sometimes she used to fumble while talking. I knew she was competing with me and she would go for another peg if I take it. So, I planned to avoid any more pegs and spend some time to know each other.

"I am flying," she said raising her arms in the air. She looked like an angel without her crown.

"You know Aaryan, I have never lived a moment like this before," said Aarushi placing her hand over mine. I got all my senses back at that very moment. Her palm was silky soft and warm. I remained static.

"Me too," I said looking at her eyes which looked far more intoxicated than any other beverages available in the bar.

"You wanted to know about me, right?" she said, taking a sip. I nodded and said, "Yes".

"Okay, from where shall I start?" she wondered.

"Why not start from your family?" I suggested.

"Hmm… Okay. Aaryan there is nothing great about my family background. You might find it very boring. I come from a place called Bulandsehar in UP. My dad…," she paused and looked at me. I could notice tears in her eyes. She was fighting with herself to restrict them. I wanted to hug her and console her for her loss, which I already knew. I placed my palm over hers and said, "It's okay. I don't force you to open up and share everything with me. I am fine even if you don't say anything to me, but I can't afford to see these tears in your eyes.". She controlled herself and smiled. I took my hands off.

"My dad and my younger brother died in a road accident when I was just 5 years old. My younger brother, Sankalp, was two years younger than me. That day, he was going with my dad on our old scooter, to get a gift for my mom. It was her birthday," continued Aarushi.

"My dad bought a beautiful red colour saree for my mom. Financially we were quite poor, but *hum dil se amir the*. My dad was a carpenter and he was the only bread earner of the family. He and my mom compromised on everything for my brother and me. He had lots of dreams and always used to say that, once my daughter becomes an IAS officer, I will die peacefully. This is quite usual with parents from UP and Bihar. They all want their kids to clear IPS or IAS. Mine were no different," said Aarushi smiling and taking a sip.

"I was playing with other kids of our locality, equally poor like us. Mom was busy in making Kheer, the sweet dish for evening. It was indeed a special day for us, as most of the days what we had as a dinner was just rice and homemade pickle. Anyway, that day, God was not at all in a mood to see us celebrating," she said with a sad tone.

There was silence in the air for the next few minutes. Aarushi was losing her battle against tears.

"He hit my dad from behind. My brother died on the spot. My father was taken to a hospital, but he died in the mid way. My mother didn't even have a chance to look at dad's body. The police said that the face was crushed and they denied showing us. The police handed the saree to my mom. Red saree for a widow!," whispered Aarushi, tears rolled down her cheeks.

"A few days later, my mom decided to log an FIR against that guy who had destroyed our happiness forever. People who witnessed the accident informed my mom, about that guy. That guy was a renowned builder's son and his dad had many contacts among the politicians. After several days of pursuing the police officer, who was stationed in our district, he finally agreed to log the FIR. He warned us not to do it or else we would be in trouble. Isn't it strange?" asked Aarushi to which I remained silent. I knew, this question was not asked to me, but she was asking herself.

"We lived in a remote area which was surrounded by agricultural lands. There were not more than 50 residents in the locality. That night, two people came to our home and knocked the door. I was having dinner, while my mom was waving the hand fan for my comfort. Hearing the knock, she went to open the door. They entered inside and locked the door. Before I could have reacted, they slapped my mom and…" paused Aarushi and started taking deep breaths. Eyes wide opened and moist.

"They tore my mother's saree into pieces. She was shouting, crying but the world was deaf. One of the guys, took me in his arms, and threatened my mom to cooperate or else, he would rape me. At that age, I didn't know, what rape meant. In fact, I was crying and saying, "Uncle, please leave me," to which he was laughing loud. Finally, my mother had to give up and she was raped in front of me. They also inserted objects in her body leaving her soaked in blood. I was crying and hitting the guy who had held me. Seeing no help, I bite his arm to which he yelled and threw me on my mom's naked body. She took hold of me and looked at me with her teary eyes. Her face and entire body was full of bruises. She wiped my tears and asked me not to cry. The guy, who raped my mom, slapped me, pulled me by my hair, punched and threw me around."

"He moved forward to pick the stove and fling on me when he received a call. They got an order from their boss to kill my mom and leave. And the next moment, they slit my mom's throat and left," said Aarushi.

Her eyes were red and she was completely frozen. A shiver ran down my spine. I could see how hard she was trying to hold herself. I didn't know what to say or how to pacify her.

"I was trying to stop blood from my mother's throat with my frock. She was dying every second. Fighting for breath. Realizing she won't survive anymore, she surfed my hair, placed my head on her chest and gripped me tight. I was crying and asking her to get up. In another few seconds, her grip was loosened. She died."

"Later, I was sent to a government orphanage, from where I did my education. Got scholarship for my higher education and kept preparing for IAS. I cleared the preliminary and moved to Noida to prepare for mains. For my livelihood, I used to give tuitions and also worked at a mall in Lucknow," said Aarushi with a little smile.

Her smile brought a little satisfaction to me.

"I have to clear the mains exam," she said relaxing herself on the sofa.

"You will clear it," I said. She looked at me, wiping her tears and smiled. The kohl in her eyes was spread, but she still looked far more beautiful than anyone one else in the club.

"Aaryan, you must promise me that you won't share this with anyone. Not even Nikhil. Also, Swati doesn't know about it. I have told her that, my mom lives in Lucknow and she is a tailor. I don't want to get anyone's sympathy," asked Aarushi extending her hand. I placed my palm over hers and promised. She blinked her eyes and said thanks.

"Okay, I think I have spoilt the night," said Aarushi looking at the dance floor where people were shaking their body like wild gorillas.

"Aarushi, can I request you something?" I asked. She nodded her head and asked me to continue.

"Please don't take me wrong," I said and gulped all the drinks available on the table, including Aarushi's. She looked at me with her angry face.

"I am sorry. But I needed it. See, the day when I saw you at the terrace, I just liked your physical appearance. I mean by your looks. A guy would either be blind or a gay not to fall for you at first sight. And I am quite sure, that you know it. You must be looking at mirrors too and moreover, the girls in your hostel," I said. She smiled as if she was agreeing to my statement.

"And it was not happening for the first time. I had liked many girls just in the first glance. But there was something special this time. You followed me everywhere. I mean not physically, but in my dreams every night, in my thoughts even when I would sit at the office desk writing some stupid codes. You never smiled at me, but I used to see your smiling face in front of me, and the best thing is, we also kissed each other once," I said raising my hands in air to showcase how glorified my imaginations could be.

Her eyes widened up and she was about to speak when I stopped her not to, "Please don't say anything. Place your finger onto your lips and seal it for a while. Let me talk. You can slap me later for this," I ordered which she followed.

"I know, this sounds stupid that how can a guy falling in love madly with a girl in just a matter of days. But, for me it is absolutely what I wanted. See, what I want to request you is forget everything that you didn't like about me. Allow me to start afresh. You have all rights to dump me at the end, but dare not to friend zone me. It's like making someone stand in front of Taj Mahal, blindfolded," I said looking at her eyes. She tried her best to stop the laugh. She covered her face with her palm and laughed silently.

"I respect you Aarushi for everything that you have faced in your life and came out of it. I wish, I could go into past and change everything as per your wish. Kill that bastard who made you face all these. Had I been in your situation, I don't know how I would have handled it. You deserve a lot more than what you have today," I said looking deep into her eyes. There was calm and serenity on her face.

"You know, sometimes, it is good to follow your heart. The problem comes when the heart starts taking opinion from the brain, which over-evaluates and complicates our life. But the best part is, my brain also has a heart and so I just take what life offers me and do what my heart says is right. And my heart said, you are right for me," I explained her.

"You asked me, what I noticed in you at the first sight," I said to which she nodded her head and leaned forward to listen to the answer.

"Would you mind if I say it in the way I love the most?" I asked for her permission. She nodded her head and passed a radiant smile.

"Aarushi, God must have gulped all the malts, before crafting your eyes, He must have revealed the best shade of pink, to color your lips, Would have thought millions of times, before embedding your name in my fortune, I may not be the best for you, but you know what God has made me, just for you," I said looking deep in her alluring eyes. Her persona conquered my heart and brain altogether. I just wanted to spend my whole life with her and give her all the happiness to compensate her past.

"Shall we dance?" she asked cleaning the mesh around her eyes.

"Who would deny dancing with a beautiful girl like you?" I said and extended my hand as a gentleman to assist her to reach the dance floor.

"Please. I can walk on my own," said Aarushi, and stood up. Well that was quite blunt.

We stood over the dance floor. The people around us were shaking as if some paranormal spirits captured their holy body. Aarushi was tapping her sandal on the floor to match the beats of DJ. Then she started shaking her head followed by hands and then the entire body. She didn't need me as a partner. She was dancing from heart, careless to be judged. She pushed, kicked and hit almost everyone who came in her vicinity. My only job at the dance floor was to say sorry to all the victims and make sure she doesn't hit her head on the dance floor. Sooner, the dance floor looked like an earthquake hit place, with Aarushi as its epicenter and people with devastated look on their face.

I realized, it was time to leave before Aarushi creates any more scenes. I booked the cab and luckily it was just a kilometre away from us.

"Aarushi, I think we should leave now," I said holding her hand and slowly pulling her off the floor. I could see a sign of relief on every aspiring horrible dancers. "Why," she said and jerked her hand to release the grip. She tried to jump over the floor again when I pushed her hard towards myself and hold her round her slim waist.

We were so close to each other that I could feel her warm breath on my face. Her hands were resting on my chest. She looked at me with her intoxicated eyes. With her eyes locked to me, I took a step closer. I wasn't sure, if my heart has ever pounded so hard in my life. There was a romantic vibe pulsating in the air. I tugged strands of her hair falling on her face behind her ears. She closed her eyes. She shivered that made her whole body trembled. Her lips, pink and soft, were shaking, sending a wild tremors down my nerves. The moment, we were about to experience our first kiss, I stopped myself.

Anticipating a kiss, she opened her eyes and looked at me. Her body was still shivering. I released my grip.

"If you were not drunk today, I could have lived the moment of my life," I said. I could notice her moist eyes.

"It was love in me and alcohol in you, which I believe, brought us so close," I said. She took a step back before I held her hand and said, "The day when I would feel like kissing you out of all my heart and express my love, I promise you, I will eat you that day," I said smilingly, to which she smiled and slapped me softly.

Our cab came and we left from the venue. Aarushi was drunk as I could see her slithering like snake. Whole way, she just kept looking outside the window and let the cool breeze play with her hair. She was smiling and that was soothing my heart. I left her in her own dreams as she looked amazingly beautiful whenever she smiled. Moonlight falling on her face made everything look divine.

I paid the bill, and helped Aarushi board off the cab. We stood in front of her hostel entry. There was no guard or warden.

She placed her hand over my shoulder and asked me to call Swati.

"I don't have her number," I said. She took her cellphone out from her purse and started looking for Swati's number.

"Your cell is switched off," I said to which she made puppy-like face.

"Shall I?" I asked unlocking the door, which made so much noise. It was definitely dying for a greasing.

"Okay," said Aarushi, and allowed me to hold her only if she falls, but she preferred to walk on her own.

Aarushi took each step cautiously as if she was expecting some land mines inside the tiles. I was following her as a guard.

"Which floor?" I asked after I noticed there was no lift. She turned back, put her hand on her waist and said making a frown face, "Don't you know?" I smiled idiotically and held my ears to say sorry.

I was about to knock the door, when Aarushi stopped me.

"Listen," she said stopping me from knocking the door.

"Thank you so much for the wonderful evening," said Aarushi smiling and looking into my eyes. I stood idle, waiting for her to say something more, like, I love you or at least she would think over it.

"I am not sure if I will ever have time to fall in love with you or for that matter anyone else, but I wish you to get the love of your choice. Don't waste your time on me. Because when you love someone, you expect the same in return. This is reality. No matter what love phrases say, they are all bullshit. So, it's better if you look for someone else, because, I may not be able to give you anything in return," said Aarushi. This time, her eyes were moist. Perhaps, because of her past she was stopping herself from falling in love.

"You will love me one day. Trust me you will. And let me promise you this," I said and held her hand, "Unless, you express your love to me, I will never say these "I love you" to you, because I already do," I said looking into her eyes. She was frozen.

"As far as expectation is concerned, I just have one expectation from you," I said to which she raised her eyebrows to ask, what? "You will not stop me from pouring my love on you. I will not be physical, I will not take any advantage of you, and I believe, you have that much trust on me," I put my condition.

"I thought, love is unconditional. You have started bombarding conditions on me in our first meet itself," said Aarushi rubbing her eyes like babies.

"The condition here is to love you. If I don't put this condition, how will I ever be able to sit next to you in an international flight for our first honeymoon," I said sarcastically with a stupid smile on my face. She smiled and all of a sudden placed her palm on her mouth and started banging the door. I took hold of her and asked her to puke.

"Don't stop it. It's okay to puke after getting drunk. It's like bleeding on the first night," I said something which I should not have had. She turned to face me and could not stop herself anymore. She puked. Nowhere else, but on my favorite shirt. For a few seconds, all I did standing there devastated was, looking at my shirt and then Aarushi, who stood there in shock.

"What the hell?" yelled Swati opening the door and after seeing the puking ceremony. "Aarushi, are you drunk?" she asked holding Aarushi in her arms and staring at me.

"A little," said Aarushi while they made move inside their room.

"Since when Starbucks started offering drinks?" yelled Swati. She was furious on me. I remained silent as one more word from me would have led to another world war. And moreover, that was not a question for which she was expecting an answer.

"It was me who asked him. It's not his fault," said Aarushi, throwing herself on the bed. She looked so innocent that I wanted to go inside the room, sit beside her and cuddle her. I got a little smile on my face just by imagining this. But, Swati could not digest my smile.

"You know what, you deserved this," said Swati pointing towards the puke banqueted over my entire shirt. I looked at my shirt and then back to her, still in my fantasies to cuddle Aarushi, I smiled. Swati could not handle my presence anymore and banged the door to close it on my face.

I reached my flat engrossed in the beautiful memory of the time spent with Aarushi. "She is too good. Not only her face, but her soul is also beautiful. I will never cheat on her," I was talking to myself. "*Kara li apni bezzati?*," taunted Nikhil opening the door. I looked at him and hugged him.

"You rascal, get away from me. Look at yourself. Look at this puked shirt," said Nikhil pushing me apart. I took the shirt off and said, "It's Aarushi's puke," with a pride smile on my face. He was shocked to see the height of my stupidity.

"I have never heard of any lover feeling proud of his partner's puke," said Nikhil lighting his cigarette. I folded my hand and requested him to give me one. He threw the packet on my face and went to the balcony. I don't remember the time, but the city was quite silent. Even dogs of our street were asleep. Except one among their species, Nikhil was awake.

"You know, she is a very nice girl," I said falling over the beanbag kept in the balcony. Nikhil looked least interested.

"I will kill that bastard," I said taking a puff. Nikhil was shocked to hear that. He turned towards me and asked, "Who? What happened tell me?" He dragged a stool and sat next to me to listen to what I said. I narrated the entire story to him.

"Do you realize whom you have threatened?" asked Nikhil quite seriously. I didn't say a word. I kept staring at the stars while I was framing a plan to kill Himanshu.

"Do you remember, once I told you that the warden of this girl's hostel has a good connection with Himanshu Joshi," said Nikhil shaking me to bring me to my senses. I looked at him, and nodded my head in acceptance.

"He misuses the political and financial power of his dad. And Salim once told me that, sometimes he takes a few girls from this hostel for his private party. And I believe, you very well understand what he must be doing with those girls in those parties," said Nikhil seriously.

"But that warden looks quite concern about the securities of those girls in the hostel," I said in favour of the warden

"She is a bitch. I think, you need to ask Aarushi to leave that hostel. It is not safe for her anymore," suggested Nikhil. I knew he made sense and was concerned about

Aarushi's safety, but I also knew that it was not that easy to convince Aarushi.

"I will talk to her. She has been through a lot. I don't want anymore difficult time for her," I said.

I could not sleep the whole night. Was wondering, what would have been the situation of Aarushi as a little girl saving her mother from barbarians. How did she manage to come out of her dark past and made it through her academics.

Most of us live a decent life, have parents to take care of us, but still we complain about life whereas this girl, without any favour from anyone, including God, struggled throughout her life and still has no complaints against anyone. What made her fall weak in front of me and share everything about her past which she didn't even share with Swati, her close friend. Was it because of alcohol or she really trusted me? I made a promise to myself that no matter what destiny has planned for me, I am going to fight all the odds and make sure that she doesn't suffer ever in her life.

To become an IAS officer was Aarushi's dream, and to love Aarushi till the last breath was my dream. In the path of life, we always get two choices, either to leave our dream or to live our dream. I chose the latter.

I wanted to ask God's favour to place all the stars in their best position so that Aarushi accept my love for her, but honestly, I never asked the almighty for any sympathy.

Chapter 13

"It was my turn"

❄ ❄ ❄

I didn't realise when I slept. My mobile alarm rang loudly.

"You stupid, when you have to wake up at 8, then why the hell you set the alarm for 7:00," yelled Nikhil, throwing a pillow on me. He looked furious. I rubbed my eyes and started looking for my cell phone. The ring tone was irritating though.

"Where is my mobile phone?" I said after I could not find it in my trousers.

"Look for it in your ass, you rascal," yelled Nikhil. This time he threw his blanket off and stood up as if he was going to jump over me and strangle me to death.

Finally, after a few more minutes and listening to the slang abuses for every member of my family, I was able to trace my mobile under the sofa cushion. I put it on silent mode and looked at Nikhil. He was still standing on his bed, confused whether to hit me or the bed. I left him in his condition and went to washroom.

In another one hour we left for our office. Mihir had left a note on my desk, *"Meet me when you are in."*

"Have you decided about your onsite," asked Nikhil switching on his laptop. I stood puzzled. I didn't want to go, but like every software engineer, I too had that onsite bug in my body, which was restricting me from taking a final decision.

"Should I ask Aarushi?" I asked Nikhil, who was already engrossed in his system. He looked at me and then asked me to come closer. I bent towards him thinking that he might give me a better suggestion, but like always he had to utter something ugly, *"Don't eat my balls,"* he whispered.

I showed him my middle finger and carried on with my work. I knew he was not at all in a good mood. After all, I had screwed his morning. Plan to call Aarushi was later dropped, as I didn't have her number.

Completely disinterested in work, I switched on my laptop and started reading spam emails. Trust me reading spam emails in office is the best way to relieve yourself from stress. And honestly, who reads spam emails at home? The subject line of most of the spams are so hilarious that you wonder that how come everyone on this planet knows that you are stupid.

"Grow your genitals in 3 easy steps."

"Congratulations! You have won GBP 300,000,000."

"Meet Meenakshi… your perfect match from Delhi."

"Dr. Batra claims to grow your hair in 2 weeks."

"Meet and have fun...no credit card required!" and thousand others. I was smiling and deleting each one of them, when Mihir called at my desk phone.

"Yes, Mihir," I said picking up the call

"Did you see the note I kept at your desk?" asked Mihir

"Yeah. I was about to come. I was helping Nikhil to understand a fix. I will be there in a few minutes," I said and hung up the call. Nikhil heard my conversation and was staring at me with anger. I gave him a flying kiss, to irritate him more. I could not hear what he said, but definitely it was nothing parliamentary and I guess, he gave a slang dedicated to my grandmother.

"Hi," I said entering Mihir's cabin. He was busy with his cellphone. He was definitely not on a call, and I believe he was browsing Facebook, as he asked me, if I was on Facebook or not.

"Let me search you on Facebook. Grab a chair," he said while he started searching me among millions of Aaryans having Facebook account.

"God, please hide my account for a minute," I silently prayed. "Who on this planet wants his manager to be in his friends list. Next time when you take a sick leave and you actually go to a bar, and upload pictures with hot girls around you, your manager will be the first person to like and comment on it. And how much he liked it will be shown in your appraisal.

"A guy with a beer pint and a nicotine stick," said Mihir looking at me for the confirmation. I nodded my head to accept the bitter truth.

"Sent," said Mihir and looked at me with a stupid smile. He gestured me to take my cellphone out and accept his friend request. I thought to myself that how stupid a person could be who after sending you friend request on a social networking site pleads you to accept his friend request. For a while, I thought of deleting my account as Mihir would definitely invade my personal space, but Facebook was an addiction. Once you create an account, it means the world to you. Helpless, I accepted his friend request.

"Accepted," I said hitting the button. Mihir smiled

and stood from his chair.

"So, shall I go now? We are now friends on Facebook," I said sarcastically.

"No. I wanted to know your decision about the onsite offer," said Mihir placing his hand over my shoulder. For a moment, I really had a doubt, if he was a gay. I was scared. I stood from my chair and said, "I thought over it, but I think, I may not be able to go. Sorry."

"What? Are you insane? Going on an onsite is a dream for all software engineers, and you are saying no to this opportunity," said Mihir moving his hands in all possible directions to show the characteristics of a hidden girl inside his male body.

"I completely understand this Mihir, but I can't opt to go at this point of time," I said. Mihir made some girly faces to show his frustration. He picked up his coffee mug poured in the hot water from his flask.

"Would you like to have some green tea?" asked Mihir.

"No, thanks," I rejected politely.

"Is there any issue you want to share? I mean, what is stopping you," he gave another attempt to convince me.

"There is nothing to share. It's just what I feel," I said without showing my emotional side.

"*Huuh*, okay. I don't want to force it on you," he said and took a sip of his green tea.

"Why don't you send Nikhil. He is a lot deserving than me," I suggested. Mihir looked and passed a wicked smile at me.

"Yeah, I know. But he is working for an Indian client," said Mihir. What really hurted me was, "Yeah, I know". I mean, how could he agree right on my face that Nikhil was more talented than me. Couldn't he keep that secret to himself. Though, it was true, but he shouldn't have said that right on my puppet face, after all, Mihir and I shared another relationship now i.e. Facebook friends.

"Okay then I will take your leave now," I said opening the door of his cabin.

"Yeah, see you," said Mihir and got busy with his cellphone.

Nikhil asked me to join him for a smoke. I knew he was more interested in knowing my decision and the discussion that happened between me and Mihir. I narrated him the whole story except the "Yeah, I know" part.

"What did he say when you proposed my name?" asked Nikhil taking a deep puff. I thought for a while to frame an answer and then said, "He said you need to be more vocal and improve your coding abilities.". Nikhil was shocked to hear that. More than shocked, he felt insulted and furious.

"Such a cheapster. I will put all the codes in his ass. Will he teach me coding? What does he know about coding? He just know how to roam around in the office with a hope that some guy would fall in love with his ass. Bastard!" yelled Nikhil in a single breath. I loved it. The best part was that he was having a bad day, and all because of me. Really, best friends are the best enemies.

After browsing and killing time for another 6 hours, we left for our room. Nikhil spent the whole day in updating his resume and uploading it at various job portals. He was really frustrated. I was feeling sorry for him, but decided to hide the truth as it could have cost me my life.

On the way, I received a message from an unknown number.

"*Sorry for yesterday. Plz give your shirt to me. Will wash it,*" read the message.

I knew it was Aarushi, for certain. I was excited to see the message. My heart beat faster than Nikhil's bike. I engaged my brain cells to think for a beautiful reply, afterall, it was my first message to her.

"Keh do to jaan de du tere chokhat par, keh dena ishq ki kurbaani hai

Lekin, kaise de du us kameez ko, jis par mere pyar ki pehli nishaani hai" I replied in my own style.

A cute little smile made its presence on Aarushi's well carved face. She replied, *"Waah Waah! Anyway, I have something for you.. Shall we go to the Krishna temple, if u r free,"*

"Another date!" my sub-conscious mind expressed. My heart knew what exactly it was going through. The feeling of being in love is amazing. Nothing can outshine it. Spending time with that special someone, whom you never knew before, but sooner you start discovering them, can't be expressed in words. I could now think why God kept me aloof from falling into any commitment. Perhaps, even God was busy writing my love story.

"What if I get you kidnapped and marry you at that temple?" I texted, adding a cunning smile at the end.

Not even a minute passed, Aarushi's message arrived in my inbox.

"Dare to do it. Next moment you will be knocking hell's door," replied Aarushi. I replied with a nerd smiley and confirmed my availability. I was available 24*7 for her, anyway.

"Bhai, today you just order dinner for yourself," I said throwing my office bag to some random corner of the hall. Nikhil looked at me with suspicion as he sensed something fishy in my behaviour. I was trying to be nice to him, which he could not digest so well.

"Why, are you going to consume poison for dinner?" blabbered Nikhil while switching on his laptop. I took a beer bottle from the refrigerator and flung it in air, "Catch," I shouted. Nikhil dived like Jonty Rhodes and caught the beer. I thought, he would ask me praise his catching abilities, but he was not at all in sportive mood.

"If it would have got broken, I swear on my mom, I would have fucked you," yelled Nikhil, rubbing his elbow which got hurt in that heroic dive. I laughed like insane.

"What makes it so funny?" asked Nikhil searching for the opener.

"Since morning, you have fucked all the members of my family, including my forefathers. It was only me who was left. And now you did that to me too," I said to which he smiled and kicked me. In friendship we never take meanings out of slangs, and if you do, then trust me, it's not the friendship which will last long.

"Where are you going for dinner?" asked Nikhil while he was updating his resume. He was still in the mental trauma and could not believe Mihir had that ridiculous opinion for him.

"Aarushi and I are going to the Krishna temple," I said hunting for a washed shirt from my wardrobe.

"Don't tell me! Are you going to get married?" asked Nikhil suspiciously.

"Wish I could. By the way, who on this holy planet said that, a girl and a guy could go to a temple, together, only if they have to marry?" I questioned him.

Nikhil passed a cunning smile and wished me all the best for my second date. I took bathe and wore a *kurta-pyjama*. Every place has a dress code defined. And I assumed that seeing me in ethnic attire, Lord Krishna would definitely listen to my prayers. We humans are so selfish, you see.

I got ready and messaged Aarushi, *"Let's go else the priest may leave."*

"Yep. I am ready. Let the priest leave and how does

it matter?" texted Aarushi.

"Don't you need someone to chant *Vedic mantras* for our wedding or you are planning to kiss me in the church and conclude our wedding," I replied with a cunning smile emoticon at the end of the message.

"Will you ever get serious? I am waiting downstairs," she blasted.

I took Nikhil's bike while he was busy searching for a suitable job among thousands of listed jobs in hundreds of job portals.

"Aaj to khuda bhi apne kabliyat par gurur karega,
Jara nazare bacha ke rakhna usse, warna
Woh bhi insaano wali bhul karega."

I said loud enough to make my gorgeous lady turn. She was dressed in a lemon yellow salwar suit with white dupatta perfectly pinned at her shoulders. She didn't require any artificial make-up, God had already done enough of her.

"Please for god sake, stop flirting with me," she said while I kick started the bike. She sat on the pillion and safely placed the hanging dupatta on her lap. I looked at her from the side mirror and smiled.

"What?" she asked.

"The rules of sitting behind me on the bike remains the same," I said with a wicked smile.

"Which rule?" she questioned with an irritating expression.

"All the bumps and potholes on the street are pure work of negligence from the government. Application of brakes to avoid accidents should be considered as a smart move. If anyone sitting at the pillion gets closer to the driver, while the later applies brake, then it should just be considered as a coincidence caused due to law of inertia.

Rider should not be held responsible for any inconvenience caused," I said sounding quite serious.

Aarushi smiled and gestured me to drive. Within ten minutes we reached the temple. I parked my bike and then we took footwear and handed it over to the sandal store. Isn't it hilarious? The very first thought that comes to almost all the devotees who go to a temple is "*What if someone steals my footwear?*"

Aarushi bought some flowers and sweets from the Prasad counter. I was just accompanying her as a shadow. I was lost in her divine beauty. A serene look on her face was such a blessing to watch.

"Hey, how are you my son?" a voice interrupted my devotion. I turned and to my shock, he was none other than the priest *Ghanshaym Ji*, who once gave me the cow dung cake. I bowed down to touch his feet.

"I am fine *Pandit Ji*," I said hiding my shocked state behind a fake smile. Aarushi too joined, and offered her greetings by touching the priest's feet.

"God bless you!" said *Ghanshyam Ji* and then looked at me and asked the question which he should not have asked.

"That day you took the cow dung for the house warming function. How was that?" he asked with a smile.

"How was the cow dung or how was the function?" I asked smiling. He pulled my cheek and said, "Very smart fellow. Okay, I will take a leave now. Jai Shri Krishna". Aarushi was smiling on the fact the she knew the whole story behind the cow dung cake.

"Listen, before I go to offer my prayers, I have something to tell you," said Aarushi adjusting flowers on her puja plate. I got quite tensed to hear that. "Does she love someone else? or did she bring me here to introduce me to her boyfriend?What if she breaks my heart? and several other bizarre thoughts stroke my brain."

"What is that?" I asked. She looked around to find a place to sit.

"Let's go there and talk," said Aarushi pointing towards a bench kept under the huge banyan tree inside the temple premises.

"This one is for you," said Aarushi and handed me an envelope. At first I thought, she had written a love letter to me, but later I found that it was a letter from the Combined Defense Services. I had a smile on my face.

"Salim received it on your behalf from the postman. He handed me saying, it belongs to Aaryan bhaiya. I am full confident that you have included him too in the conspiracy," said Aarushi beaming, while I was judiciously slashing the envelope. I looked at her and passed a cunning smile to confirm Salim's involvement in my strategy to make Aarushi fall in love with me.

"God, I am selected. I have been called for the SSB interview in Mysore!" I jumped with thrill. Aarushi too was happy to see me in that state of happiness. She stood to congratulate me.

"You are such a lucky star for me," I said and hugged her. Yes, I hugged her! For a moment neither of us could realize what happened, but soon when I noticed Aarushi's frozen state, I loosened the grip and stood in front of her like an innocent baby. She looked at me and said, "Last warning". I nodded my head to accept.

"I am happy for you. So now you will soon become an officer in the Indian Air Force," said Aarushi

"Hope so. But this is my third attempt. I had tried earlier too, but was not able to clear the SSB interview. It's very tough. It's not like engineering entrance exams where you can prepare yourself for a few months and clear it. For clearing SSB you have to be what you are. I mean, the officers who take interview can easily judge you if you are faking or not," I said in a gloomy tone, realizing the hard truth of SSB interviews. Aarushi looked at me and smiled.

"So, you are afraid of rejection," she questioned me.

"Yes I am. And you will not understand as you have never faced a rejection," I said bluntly. Aarushi looked at me and sneered.

"I have lived a life of rejection," whispered Aarushi. Her eyes got moist. I felt like biting my tongue. I lost words to comfort her. I never had an intention to hurt her, I was only trying to convey my failures in life, but I chose wrong words.

"I am sorry, I never meant to hurt you. Please," I said holding my ears and asked for forgiveness.

"Please don't do this. I am fine and I can understand your situation," she said asking me to take my hand off my ears.

"You know, I was born and brought up at Pathankot in Punjab. We have an Indian Air Force station in Pathankot. Those fighter jets, their engine sound, these things used to fascinate me. And moreover, the uniform of the Air Force is the best. I always wanted to see myself attired in the Air Force uniform with shining bands over my shoulder and medals on my chest. But, not all dreams can be achieved. As most of the engineering students, I too landed up in the software industry, where all you do is write some stupid codes, fix bugs which you only introduced in your code and wait for the year end to get that extra penny in your pay slip," I gave my reasons.

"Jinke sapne asmaan chune ke the, woh zameen par hi fanaa ho gaye."

"You know, sometimes I really think that how can someone say shayari with a drop of a hat," said Aarushi. She was amazed to see my talent. I raised my collar to show off.

"Wait, I didn't say I like them. So don't try to behave as if you have impressed me with your stupid two liners," she poked.

"You are so jealous of my talent. Don't worry I will train you too after our wedding," I said to which she gave a go-to-hell kind of gesture.

"You know, you should not be afraid of failing in life, because that is the only moment where you discover the real you. You said that you failed in earlier attempts, and I am sure, you know the reason. Don't you?" asked Aarushi looking into my eyes. It was tough for me to lie to her.

"Yes I do. I lied to almost every question asked to me by the interviewer. I thought that it would make the interviewer believe that I am a suitable candidate," I said in my defense.

"This time, be honest. Don't fake as it doesn't last long," she advised.

I looked at Aarushi and smiled to accept her guidance.

"There is one thing more that I want to say," said Aarushi tucking strands of hair behind her ears.

"Are you in love with me?" I said to which she made a clinical face and asked me to shut up.

"My mains exam is in another three weeks. It's on August 3, which is a Tuesday," said Aarushi enthusiastically.

"That's good. But why do you look so happy for that. Exams nearing always give a headache to me, and you feel so good about it," I said.

"It gives you headache because you are afraid of getting failed. And I am excited because I will fulfil my dreams soon,"she said.

She is such an inspiration for me. I never looked at my life as positive as her. She was so sure about her success that she never worried about the failure. And in my case,

I would start framing the excuses for failure which might come in future before even preparing to achieve success.

"Thank you for your honest feedback," I sighed.

"So, when is your interview?" asked Aarushi.

"I have to be present at Mysore campus on August 2. I will have to be there for another four days, if I clear the first day exam," I answered her.

"So you are leaving a day before my exam," said Aarushi. I looked at her to check if she was happy for that or sad. She didn't look happy, which gave a pleasant feeling to my heart.

"You must be happy that you won't see me on your special day," I told her.

Aarushi looked at me and smirked. She thought for a while and said, "There is no doubt that I hated you at the first sight. You were like one among those eve teasers roaming on the streets watching every passing girl. But after meeting and knowing a little bit about you, I realized you are stupid, idiot, but not a kind of guy who is selfish or has any wrong intention."

I smiled and it was for the first time that I liked being called stupid and idiot and other synonyms attached to these words.

"Aarushi, I was just wondering if you ever had a boyfriend," I asked keeping my fingers crossed. She looked at me and said, "Does it matter to you?"

"Not really, but yeah somewhere it does. As a prospective lover, I should be aware about your likes and dislikes to avoid my chances of rejection," I answered bluntly.

"I love reading. I love books. I fall in love with the characters of history. I wonder how they managed their emperor so well without any bell curve or doing any SWOT analysis. There is a lot to learn from the world's history," said Aarushi in a fascinating manner.

I was shocked to hear that. How can someone fall in love with history books?

"It seems you don't like history?" asked Aarushi after she saw my disinterested face.

"Nope. Not at all. I believe in creating one," I said folding sleeves of my kurta.

"Please, don't use your vocal skills to hide your weakness," she blasted.

"At least, you agree that I have vocal skills. And by the way, when I asked you about your likes and dislikes, I didn't mean Aurangzeb or Babar. I wanted to know what makes you happy. What is that you love doing?" I rephrased my question.

"I don't know yet. I am yet to have a happy moment in my life. But it doesn't mean I am sad or depressed. It's just that, being an orphan, I have lost so much in my life that I am still fighting to come out of it. And maybe once I fulfil my dad's dream, I will realize what happiness is," said Aarushi. Her eyes glittered with the moon's reflection.

"I understand. And I am sure you will get it through. But tell me, why did you want to come to temple? Bribe God to help you in clearing mains," I said to bring a lighter moment in our discussion.

Aarushi smiled and said, "Yeah, it has been too late. The bribe is still on my plate. Let's go," said Aarushi asking me to join her in puja.

"I will wait for you outside. You go," I said.

"Don't you want to bribe God for your SSB interview?" taunted Aarushi.

"Jo maang ke mile,
Woh uphaar kaisa,
Jo maangne pe de,
Woh bhagwaan kaisa," I said in my style. She said "*Waah waah*" and asked me to wait outside while she is

back.

"Hey wait," I said.

"What" she said and stopped on the stairs to listen to me. I went near her, and placed her dupatta to cover her head. She could not say anything.

"Now, you look complete," I said stepping back.

"Don't you want to pray?" she asked me.

"My prayer is already done," I said pointing my hands towards Aarushi. She smiled and went inside to offer her prayers. Meanwhile, I spent my time re-evaluating the call letter of my SSB. I could not believe that I got another chance to live a life of my choice. Aarushi's inspirational talk was striking my brain every second.

"How will I look dressed in Air Force attire?" I was imagining myself walking in the uniform with my badges and a Ray-Ban sunglass over my eyes. I took the leverage of my imagination and created a handsome personality out of me. I was smiling on my own, when Aarushi shook me to reality.

"Where are you lost?" she asked giving me a flower, which she received from the priest as blessing.

"Are you proposing me?" I said beamingly. Aarushi looked at me and laughed.

"Please stop flirting inside the temple. This flower is just for your good luck. Keep it with you when you go for your interview," she said and gave me a *ladoo.*

"Now please don't ask if this *ladoo* is a proof that I am happy to have you in my life or anything nonsense like that. It is just a *prasad*," said Aarushi making everything clear from her end.

"Why you didn't give me the rose? At least it would have been a dress-rehearsal for you to propose me," I said pointing at the red rose in her flower basket.

"Come out of your dreams Mr Java. Sorry, but I

love roses. I can't give it to you," she said hiding the only rose in her basket with her dupatta.

"Peete rahe jam zindagi bhar, (They kept drinking entire life)

jinhe mohabbat sharaab se hai, (Who were in love with alcohol)

Hum to kaanto ki tarah, unki aankhon mei dhondte rahe pyar, (As a thorn, I kept waiting for love in the eyes of those)

Jinhe mohabbat gulaab se hai" (who were in love with rose)

"*Kuch bhi,*" said Aarushi smiling over my shayari. I sighed.

"Hey, shall we go out for dinner?" I asked while collecting our sandals from the counter.

"Just hold this for a while," said Aarushi handing me her puja basket while she struggled to wear her sandals.

"May I help you?" I asked her.

"No thanks, I can manage. It's the strap, which is broken. I need to get it fixed," said Aarushi fixing the strap. Her sandal was broken, but unlike other girls she didn't mind coming out with it.

"I think you need to replace them with a new one," I said. Aarushi smiled and asked me to get the bike.

We decided to have dinner at Salim's shop as Aarushi was not comfortable going out. But I knew, she didn't deny for a good restaurant because of her mental comfort, but it was because of her financial strength to afford lavish dinner. I didn't force her and anyway, what could have been the best place to have dinner other than Salim's shop, my co-conspirator!

"Are Bhaiya-Bhabhi ek sath!" said Salim ecstatically folding his hands to greet us. The bhabhi word though smoothened my heart, but didn't go well with Aarushi. She

was shocked to hear that.

"Salim bhai, I am not your bhabhi. We are just friends," explained Aarushi

"What? You promised that you won't friend-zone me," I yelled. Salim was looking at both of us, confused how to intervene.

"Fine, we are not friends. But I am not your bhabhi," said Aarushi convincing Salim. Like a robot, Salim nodded his head to agree

"You could have ended your statement with, yet," I said to which Aarushi made a frustrated look and sat over a chair out of irritation. Salim looked at me and asked, "What next?". I gestured him to keep quiet and bring the menu.

"She is not your bhabhi yet. But one day she will," I said proudly to Salim. Aarushi looked at me and said, "What the hell are you guys up to? Can't we just have dinner and go," asked Aarushi.

I remained silent and gestured Salim to bring the menu. Salim, with a nervous smile on his face came with the menu card and handed it to me.

"*Bhabhi ko do,*" I said and before Aarushi would have taken her sandal out to throw it on my face, I reframed my statement, "*Madam ko do.*"

Aarushi picked up the menu card and started looking for options. Meanwhile, I decided to message the astrologer to ask if she was alive or dead.

"*Hey, where are you now-a-days. No guidance at all. I am sitting with Aarushi at the shop opposite to my flat. She is furious on me. What shall I do to make her comfortable?*" I messaged to the lady astrologer. I got a reply in just a matter of seconds. I doubted if I was the only customer she had.

"*You are an idiot. You made that girl drink. And moreover you got her roommates scooty towed to a police station,*" texted Swati, the lady astrologer. I was shocked to read that message. "*How the hell does she know about that incident?*" I asked to myself.

"The scooty which you drive to Starbucks that day belonged to you or Swati?" I asked Aarushi, while she was placing order to Salim. Aarushi raised her eyebrows in surprise as how did I guess it.

"The scooty that you got towed for fun, belonged to Swati. How can I afford a scooty? And moreover, the dress, which I wore for the club, and you, praised also belonged to Swati," said Aarushi looking at me wondering why was I even asking these questions to her.

Aarushi's reply increased my belief in the lady astrologer. "She has some direct connection with God. How the hell would she know that the scooty belonged to Swati," I murmured to myself.

"*I didn't do it intentionally. And honestly her roommate exaggerates everything. She is a moron. Leave her. Tell me how long will it take for Aarushi to accept my love,*" I texted while Aarushi was staring me. I looked at her and smiled to hide my nervousness.

"What are you doing?" asked Aarushi after catching me hiding my cellphone.

"Nothing. Just playing message-message," I replied. She didn't say anything.

"Do you go to tuitions?" I asked to change the topic.

"No. I don't need it. I have sufficient time to prepare myself," she said playing with her colorful bangles.

"Is it because, you don't have enough money to afford one," I asked. She looked at me with anger and said, "I have enough money to afford books," I was meek and quiet to hear that.

My cell phone beeped to notify me a new message. I looked at Aarushi for her permission to read the message. Aarushi looked at me and said, "What? It's your mobile.

Why are looking at me. Play message-message," taunted Aarushi. I gave a quick look at the message, which read

"How dare you call her a moron? She is the only girl who can get you to Aarushi. Dare not say this again. And don't message me now or else, I will destroy your semi baked love story," read the message.

I never liked when she threatened to destroy my love story. This was a sort of blackmailing. I took a pledge that once Aarushi accepts my love, I will send a message to the stubborn astrologer saying, *"Fuck off."*

Meanwhile, Salim placed all the items ordered by Aarushi for dinner. *Dal makhni, Bhindi hara bhara and tandoori roti.*

"*Bhindi* (lady finger)!I hate *bhindi*. Who the hell eats *bhindi*?" I yelled without realizing that Aarushi ordered it. She looked at me with shrunken eyebrows.

"When I was placing the order, you were indulged in your cell phone. Now when I have ordered what I like, you have an issue. And moreover, ladies finger contains lots of vitamins, calcium, iron..." she started lecturing like a mother.

"Stop, stop, stop," I interrupted the lady who took the insult of ladies finger quite personally. "I thought we will have non-veg," I suggested.

"I am a vegetarian. If you want you can order," said Aarushi taking her first bite. Salim was standing there as a silent spectator. I looked at Salim and gestured him to leave, but he had some more innovative plans to get me screwed further.

"Shall I dim the lights and place a candle on the table. It will be romantic," said Salim hoping to get praised for his creative idea. Aarushi stopped half way to take her second bite and looked at me. She looked so frustrated that I was scared she might throw that dal makhni on me.

"*Bhai, tu ja* (Please go). This is enough for today," I said asking Salim to go. Salim, though didn't look happy with our decision, made a move.

"Who else in this locality knows that I am your girl friend?" asked Aarushi showing me the fork in her hand. I looked at her and took a pause and quickly grabbed the fork from her hand.

"Except you, everyone. I mean, Nikhil, Swati, Salim, a few of the neighbours who caught us together and the kids whom Nikhil and I provide lunch during the weekends," I said with a pride.

"Even the kids?" said Aarushi who was shocked to hear that. I nodded as a shameless guy to say yes. She sighed. I kept eating to avoid direct eye contact.

For another ten minutes we didn't say anything until, I remembered my discussion with Nikhil where he asked me to suggest Aarushi for leaving the hostel.

"Shall I say something," I asked for permission. Aarushi looked at me with a fake smile and said, "Would you not if I don't permit?"

"It's quite important so it doesn't matter actually," I said smiling to make her mood light.

"It should better be good or else I still have one spare fork with me," said Aarushi pointing the fork at me.

"Himanshu is not a good guy," I started. "He organizes some private parties where he takes girls from your hostel," I explained to her.

"What? Are you insane? Haven't you seen our hostel warden?" yelled Aarushi.

"She is a bitch," came a sound from behind, Salim was hiding behind the curtains to give us some space, but he was hearing our conversation all this time.

I looked behind and asked him to come out. Salim stood there with a shameful expression as he was caught red handed.

"Come here, grab this chair," said Aarushi passing a chair to Salim. I was wondering if I should continue eating or I should get seriously involved in the discussion.

"Bhabhi, I know that warden," started narrating Salim. Before Aarushi would have slapped Salim for calling her Bhabhi, I interrupted.

"*Sale tu marwayega aaj* (You will get me killed today, you rascal)!" I warned Salim.

"Okay sorry," said Salim holding his ears. Aarushi asked him to release his ears, but Salim looked at me for final approval. I looked at him quite seriously and said, "*Pakda reh* (keep holding). It suits you."

"Tell me what do you know," asked Aarushi wiping her hands.

"Your warden and Himanshu are quite close. She takes a few girls from the hostel for the private party at Himanshu's guest house. And after getting them drunk, she is the one who shoots their videos when Himanshu and his friends get physical with those girls. Thereafter, girls are warned not to log a police complaint or else their video would go viral. Some girls, compromise but there was a girl who could not," narrated Salim. Aarushi and I were shocked to hear that. How can a woman do something shameful like this?

"Who was that girl and what did she do?" asked Aarushi.

"Divya. She was a medical student at AIIMS. She was the one who told me about all these. She pleaded to your warden, but all went in vain. As she was quite beautiful, she became the first choice of Himanshu. One day she decided to leave the hostel and go to some other place where she won't be caught. She left the hostel early morning. I arranged the cab for her. I never asked where she was going and neither did she say anything about her plans. A few days later, she committed suicide. Her MMS was sent across almost all the students of AIIMS," said Salim. His eyes were moist.

Aarushi lost the battle to control her tears. "I can imagine what Divya might have gone through," she said.

He was not Himanshu who was the reason behind Divya's suicide, but us. Himanshu did create the MMS, but who was the audience? Why no one dares to fight against it? What pleasure does it give to watch the MMS of some girl getting raped? Why don't people think, that someday, the girl in the video can be their sister or daughter too? Would they also behave the same way they did with Divya? There is no point in lighting a candle for justice when there is no spark in our heart to come out of this immaturity and fight along with the victim until she or he gets the justice.

"I read about that incident. I never knew she belonged to this hostel. Neither did anyone tell me about this, not even Swati," wondered Aarushi.

"No one can dare to share it with anyone. You joined this hostel recently and due to elections approaching up, Himanshu avoids organizing his party as it may attract media and it will cost his dad's political image. Aaryan Bhaiya is correct; you should leave this hostel as soon as you can," suggested Salim.

I looked at Aarushi to know her thoughts. I knew Aarushi was not a kind of girl who would run away from problems, as all she did in her life was to fight against odds.

"This is such a shame. I will talk to Swati today. I will get that bastard behind the bars," pledged Aarushi. I was quite tensed to hear that. I thought she would look for some other place, but she was planning something that could be too dangerous for her.

"Aarushi, your exams are nearing and only thing you should be doing now is prepare yourself for it. I will find a better place for you so that you are secured," I suggested to an aspiring IAS officer.

"Why should I be concerned about my safety? You know, this is the problem in our country. Those who have not done anything wrong are worried about their safety and the ones who commit crimes roam fearless. Why do I need to be worried? What wrong have I done? Worst that may happen to me is that I would die; what wrong can someone do to me? Until I am alive, I will fight," said Aarushi.

I could see anger in her eyes. Salim and I were silent as there was no point convincing Aarushi. And what else we could have told her. She was not wrong.

"I am with you. No matter what your plan is, but I am in," I said looking into Aarushi's eyes and giving her an assurance that she won't be alone in her fight.

Aarushi smiled and thanked me for the support.

"Fine, then I will talk to Swati today and will plan our next step," said Aarushi taking out her wallet to pay the bill.

"I will pay," I said.

"None of you need to pay. Consider your first date on me," said Salim with pride on his face. I literally wanted to laugh. I knew, Aarushi was going to kick him anyway for his stupid statement, so I remained silent and waited for Aarushi's reply.

"Here is the amount. Keep it," said Aarushi while keeping the money she had already calculated before ordering the dinner. I stood up from the chair and added the remaining amount from my wallet. I kept all the money inside Salim's pocket.

"Thanks. The food was really good," said Aarushi while leaving. I wished I could have said the same thing about the food.

"And by the way, please don't talk about our first date.

It was awful," said Aarushi and walked away. Salim looked at me with a shocking face. I could not judge whether it was an insult to me or something else. I ran behind to catch her.

"Hey, it was not awful. I thought, you had a great time," I said hoping that she would correct her statement. She stopped near her hostel gate and said, "It was awful. And I am going to say it to everyone, whosoever knows about it," with a smile on her face. I knew she was just trying to have fun of me.

"If that is the case, then first tell it to your heart. I bet it won't get convinced by your lie," I said tucking the strands of hair falling on Aarushi's face, behind her ears. She froze. Our eyes were locked to each other and we remained in that state until, Swati yelled from the balcony, "Come on guys, I want to see a kiss!"

Aarushi was traumatized to get caught by Swati and more than shock, she felt shy about it, which was an encouragement for me.

"Jo mohabbat tere dil mei hai,
Kaash tere zubaan pe hoti,
Galti teri nahi, Khuda ki hai,
Kaash dil ko jubaan di hoti"

A cute little smile on Aarushi's face gave a pleasant satisfaction to my heart. Gone were the days, when she used to hate my shayaris and my presence. We stood there for a couple of minutes without saying a word.

"Bye," said Aarushi as she could not afford to stand anymore and ran towards stairs.

"Hey listen, please say sorry to Swati on my behalf," I shouted. Aarushi stopped to listen.

"Why? Is it because she caught us?" she confirmed.

"Not at all for that reason. In fact she should say sorry to us for spoiling our mood," I said making a puppy face to show how bad I felt about that 'kiss-miss'. Aarushi showed me her palms and gestured to slap me.

"Then for what reason do you want me to say sorry to Swati?" asked Aarushi.

"Honestly even I don't know why do I need to say sorry to her, but it seems she holds quite an important role in deciding my love story," I said wondering why the hell lady astrologer asked me to say sorry.

"You are really an insane. Sometimes I don't understand you," said Aarushi running over the stairs.

"Good night" I shouted, though I could not see her, but the reply came, "See you tomorrow."

Chapter 14
Day 4

* * *

"Aaryan, you should sleep now," said Ali sir. I was up whole night. My eyes turned red, body was tired, but heart refused to rest. I kept writing whole night under the scattering light from the lamp post which was opposite to my cell.

"A few more hours sir, please. After that I will sleep forever, and promise you, I won't wake up no matter how bad you hit me with your baton," I said smiling and pointing towards the baton he was holding in his hand.

"Aaryan, I have been in this service for the past eleven years and I never felt this helpless before. I am sure you are a victim of a bad time. You don't look to me a murderer or a rapist. I don't know how I will be able to stand and witness you getting hanged tomorrow," said Ali Sir looking into my eyes for an answer. I stood up and went near to him.

"Sir, I am a murderer by choice. I murdered Himanshu brutally. I chopped his entire body into pieces. I had Himanshu's blood all over my body. I laid down beside his

chopped body and trust me at that moment of time and even now I feel good about it. I have no regrets," I replied.

Ali Sir could see anger in my eyes. He paused for a minute and then asked the question to which I had no answer.

"And what about the rape allegation against you? Did you rape that girl?" asked Ali Sir holding my hand. I could not face him and bowed my head down.

"Say Aaryan. I want to hear this from you. Why don't you understand, if you don't talk, things won't change. I want to know what happened exactly. Himanshu was a big shot guy and I know that how power influences our judicial system. I smell something fishy in your case. What do you think, the judge doesn't know the truth? But the law has bounded it's hands because of the political pressure. He has to go by the witnesses and books of laws. But today, I am not asking you as a jailor, but as your friend. Please tell me the truth," said Ali Sir.

I could easily sense the frustration in his voice. He wanted me to speak up, but I was speechless. I remained silent for a moment and then walked away from him. I took a bowl of water from the earthen pot and washed my face. I had grown beard and I badly wanted a mirror to look at myself.

"Ali Sir, is it possible if I can get my beard shaved and get a mirror tomorrow morning to make sure I am look handsome before I get hanged? I don't want angels in the heaven to make faces when I knock their door," I said by changing the topic. Ali Sir looked at me with a grin on his face as he knew I was not going to answer his question. He sighed and left. I felt bad for him, but I had no other option.

I piled up all the papers which I wrote and arranged them in a serial order. I did some stretching exercise to relax my body and prepared myself for the last writing session. I had to complete my story and I was only left with less than twenty-four hours.

I took Aarushi's photo in my hand to admire her serene face. I felt like she was talking to me through her expressive eyes. She was unique in her own way. As I was nearing my death, every memory of hers flashed in front of my eyes. Those inspirational things she would say to inspire me, her beautiful thoughts, her guts to fight against all odds, her smile to pacify my heart, her dreams to shine as an IAS officer, her strands of hair which she used to gently tug behind her ears, her nose ring which used to shine on her face like a full moon, I kissed her photo softly and kept it inside my pocket. I looked at the sky which was covered with dark clouds. "Clouds during winter, I wondered. It was very rare to see clouds in Delhi during winter.

"Hey, I know you are watching me from behind the clouds. Must be waiting for me, right? You must be happy to see me like this. What crime did I do? Aarushi is struggling for her life in the hospital, wondering if she would be able to see the next day or not. Are you taking a revenge on me just because I never asked you for anything and never offered you anything to make you happy? I am coming soon to see you and you better be ready to answer all my questions," I warned the Almighty, staring at the sky.

"Aaryan, you have got visitors," informed Manoj, the guard. I looked at him and asked him about the visitors.

"Your mom, dad and that guy who usually comes along with them," answered Manoj giving himself a tough fight to recollect the name of the guy, 'Nikhil'.

"He is my friend, Nikhil," I said dusting my shirt.

"Right, Nikhil, quite a fancy name. In our village, we keep simple names like Ram, Shayam, Ramesh, Suresh, Mahesh. It's easy to pronounce and remember," said Manoj unlocking the cell.

"Recently, I came to know the name of Facebook CEO, Mark Juka… No Mark Hukka.. Something like burger..

What the hell was that!" struggled Manoj to pronounce the name of FB CEO. It was quite a fun to look at him.

"Its Mark Zuckerberg," I helped. He sighed.

"You know if he would have been a Bihari, we would have called him as 'Are Mark-wa, bahut paisa kama rahe hai be' (Oh Mark-wa, you are making hell lots of money)," said Manoj and laughed loudly. I too joined him to encourage his sense of humour. In Bihar it's common to add a suffix, 'wa' at everyone's name. I believe only Steve Waugh and Mark Waugh, two excellent cricketers from Australia, would not feel offensive from Biharis.

After a few more irrelevant discussions on the pronunciation of complicated names, we reached the visitor's area. I stopped before entering the lobby to see what they were doing.

I saw my mom wiping off her tears, while my dad was holding her tight, perhaps asking her to control herself. Nikhil was standing quietly with a tiffin box in his hand. My mom took out "Hanuman Chalisa" from a little purse she carried. They looked so helpless, and by seeing their faces I could easily judge that they had not slept for long. I could understand their pain of losing the only son that had. It was going to be the last meet for us as the next day they would only get to see my dead body and recall the memories.

"Aaryan, I can understand what you and your family would be going through. But you don't have enough time allotted for this meeting. I think you should go and meet them," said Manoj when he saw me in tears.

"Yeah, you are right. I don't have much time," I said and wiped my tears. I entered the lobby with a smile on my face to make my parents comfortable.

I folded my hands to offer my greetings to them. My mom saw my handcuffs and then stared at Manoj. She knew that Manoj won't free my hands. I looked at mom and said,

"Oh ho, why are you worried about these handcuffs. I am in front of you, isn't that enough?"

She passed her fingers from the grill to touch my hands. I touched her fingers to comfort her. My dad was standing, tough and steady, fighting to control his emotions. I looked at him and asked him to relax as everything was fine. I could notice their red eyes which proved that they had been crying all these days for me. We didn't speak anything for another few minutes. We were just looking at each other. All the memories of my childhood flashed in front of my eyes. The way my mom used to feed me with her hands, my dad who used to run in between the rooms, with me sitting on his shoulders, the scolding and slaps I used to get for my notorious activities, my birthday celebrations when my mom used to spend the whole day in cooking delicious food for the night,, and many more. Soon, I could not control my tears and broke. "What would happen to my parents after I am gone?", I burst into tears. They were growing old and I was worried about who would take care of them in their old age.

"I am sorry. Please forgive me," I said crying like insane. By this time, all of us had lost the battle to control our tears from showing up. We badly wanted to hug each other, the last time. But all our feelings and emotions died in our heart as there was nothing we could have done to realize our last wish. Nikhil tried to pacify my parents and looked at me with teary eyes.

"Why are you doing this Aaryan? Why don't you speak up? Why do you want to leave us forever?" said Nikhil shaking the grill. Manoj wanted to warn Nikhil for his behaviour, but he stopped himself when I pleaded him not to say anything.

"Nikhil, tell me who is going to believe me? There are no witnesses and no proof to prove my innocence. We live in a country where, if you have power and money, you can

warn witnesses to give their statement in court and you can modulate proves as per your wish. What will happen even if I shout that I was not guilty? Who is going to believe me? The court needs proofs and witnesses to decide my guiltlessness. I am helpless, please understand," I cried. There was nothing that I lied, they too knew whatever I was saying was the fact and they could not deny it.

My mom wiped her tears and said, "Nothing will happen to you. Don't worry. You are not guilty and god will save you." She was not assuring me, but herself. She passed the Hanuman Chalisa (Holy book of hindus) through the grill and asked me to recite it seven times so that God would save me from my already decided fate. I smiled and took it.

"Beta, there is a lot of hatred outside for you. Everyone wants you to be hanged. It's tough for us to convince your innocence to everyone. I don't know how we will be able to face tomorrow's day, when one side, we will be shattered to see you dead and the other side the whole country would celebrate your death. I don't have enough strength to face all these. Knowing that you are not guilty, makes it even more tougher for us," expressed dad.

The world outside was waiting for me to be hanged. For them I was the one, who raped a girl who loved me so much. Media was covering everything, which could have raised their viewership. I was quite famous outside, but for wrong reasons. Every mouth that opened asked for 'Justice to Aarushi'. Slogans were raised, banners were made, and candle march was being organised to support Aarushi and wish her quick recovery. I was happy to hear all these from Nikhil. At least, Aarushi was getting millions of wishes for her recovery.

But out of all this, what surprises me is that where were these millions of eyes, when Aarushi was raped and thrown to die? Why no one saw her lying on the floor when she was bleeding? Why no one bothered to call an ambulance and get her to hospital? Why on that day, everyone turned blind, deaf and dumb? Where were these people then? We blame, organise strike, but when are we going to be responsible enough to stand for such heinous crimes against women. Standing against rape is much more cheaper than buying a candle for a march. But in our country, buying a candle is cheaper than saving someone's life. It requires courage, but most of us are cowards, we ourselves let crime happen and then show our sympathies by joining candle march.

"Papa, don't worry. Things will be all right. And why do you need to worry about what others think of me? You know the truth, and you don't need to convince anyone to accept it. You all accept that I am not guilty and that is enough for me to die peacefully. You just take care of yourself and ma. That is all I want. And Ma, please don't cry. At least you will be able to hug me tomorrow. You will be able to have me on your lap and love me as much as you want. There will be no one to stop you," I said clutching the grills. It was tough for all of us to accept that it was our last meet. My mom begged to Manoj and cried when the later came to notify me about the time. Manoj agreed to give two more minutes to live our last moments.

"Beta, I prepared your favourite dessert," said Mom taking the tiffin from Nikhil. I could see a satisfaction in her eyes.

"Is it besan ke laddoo (a type of sweet)?," I asked with an excitement. I gestured Manoj to join. Though, my mom was not happy to share the laddoo with Manoj.

"Ab sab yehi khaa jayega (Now he will only eat all the laddoos)," taunted Mom in a very low tone which could not reach Manoj's ear drum. I looked at Mom and smiled. Manoj took two pieces of laddoos and said thanks. My mom was not expecting Manoj to take out two from the tiffin; frustrated she looked at me. I gestured her to calm down. She turned her face

away to show her frustration.

"I think the time is over Aaryan. You should leave now," said Manoj. He didn't even realize he was standing there with the laddoos prepared by my mom, who was not at all happy when I shared the laddoos with Manoj. My mom got furious on Manoj's statement and yelled, "See, I told you. You thought he was a good man. Just after taking the laddoo he is asking us to leave."

Manoj could not understand what happened and stood confused, looking at me for a clarification. He was not sure whether to eat the laddoos or return them.

"Mom, please stop this. He is just doing his job. And moreover he has asked me to leave not you," I pacified my mom.

"What will we do here, once you leave? And doesn't he understand that this is the last time we are seeing you? Once you leave, you are never going to come back," replied Mom and this time she could not control her tears. She cried insanely. It was tough for all of us not to shed tears as somewhere we all realised that the time was over and I had to leave.

"Nikhil, will you do me a favour," I asked him.

"Sale, from when have you started asking me for a favour? You think our friendship is over that's why you are acting so formal?" replied Nikhil angrily. I smiled back at him to make him calm.

"You remember you promised me that if I get Aarushi in my life you will do whatever I ask you to do?" I asked reminding him to the commitment he made to me.

"Yeah, I do. Say what you want me to do," he asked me.

"I am writing a story about everything that happened since I saw Aarushi. It has the good times as well as the bad ones. I want to get the book published. Tomorrow, when you all come to collect my body, please don't forget to ask for my

book from Ali Sir," I said.

My parents were just looking at me without saying a single word. Perhaps they were trying to register my last memories in their heart.

"Do I have a place in your book? It better be or else, I will publish it on my name," said Nikhil.

"Though, you don't deserve a place in my book, but I have included you too just for the sake of having a side actor," I taunted. Nikhil smiled and nodded to fulfil his promise.

I looked at the big round clock placed inside the visitor's area. The needles of the clock appeared to move faster to warn me that my end was near. I stood from the stool and folded my hands to offer my last greetings to my parents. My body shivered just by the thought of leaving them forever. Tears refused to stop, body froze.

"I have to go. Please don't cry. A rapist and a murderer deserve this punishment. The world outside is happy because for the first time they are witnessing a proper judgement. I just want a respect for me in your eyes, and that's all I need for me to die peacefully. Don't compromise on your health worrying about me. I am not going to leave you alone. I will always be around you. And please do take care of Aarushi. She has seen enough of bad times in her life. I don't want her to have any more of those. And I have a strong belief that she will survive, because she is a fighter. She can't give up, never," I said while the tears refused to stop.

"Please don't leave us beta, please don't go. Aaryan, look at me, please," cried my mom. She was shaking the grill hard and crying loudly to make me turn and see her once. It became tough for me to turn back and look at the wretched condition of my parents. But, it was even tougher to step out of the visitor's area knowing that, I would never come back again to see them. Manoj could see the level of sorrowness in my parent's eye. He gestured me to turn back and look at

them once. I took a deep breath to gather enough strength to see my parent's for the last time and offer my final greetings. With tears still flowing through my eyes, I folded my hand and bowed my head to take their blessings. I could understand how tough it would be for parents to look at their son, whom they nurtured with utmost care and affection, for the last time. Tomorrow no matter how badly they would want me to come back, I would not. Dead bodies don't react."

I could not make it to face them for another second and left. The hue and cry of my parents echoed everywhere in the jail premises until my parents were asked to leave and come tomorrow to collect my body. My mom fainted just by the thought of having my dead body on her lap. Somehow when she came back to senses, my dad made her realize the hard truth and pleaded her to gather strength for the tough time which they were going to witness soon.

I wanted to cry my heart out inside the cell. I was not afraid of being hanged to death, but it was the memories of my parents which made it tough for me to remain calm. Realizing that I won't get any extra day to live, I wiped my tears and started to pen down the final chapters of my life.

Chapter 15
The FIR

* * *

A few more days passed and our exams came nearby. Aarushi used to study the whole day and would never reply to my messages. Sometimes, I used to feel bad because of her negligence. But later she explained me, how badly she wanted to achieve her dreams. I too realized how important her dream was for her. The reason she never replied to my messages was it would have encouraged me to talk more which would affect her studies. But nevertheless, she used to make up all my misunderstandings at Salim's shop where we used to meet every evening.

She used to hand me her general knowledge book and would ask me to randomly ask her questions, to which I put up a condition that with every wrong answer, she would say Í Love You' to me. But, she was so thorough with the current affairs that my ears never got an opportunity to hear those three beautiful words from her.

Sometimes, Salim, too, used to jump in between

and suggest me some tough questions, but Aarushi would always give correct answers to all the questions. Though, I could not make her say, I love you, but somewhere I too wished her to answer all the questions. I was falling in love with the smile she used to have after every correct answer. I could not have asked for more.

It was July 31, and the next day I had to leave for Mysore for my SSB interview. I had not informed Mihir about my leave plans as I knew he won't approve. He was not at all in a good relation with me after I denied the offer to go on an onsite project.

Aarushi had decided to take things forward and talk to Swati for more details about the connection between Himanshu and her hostel warden. Honestly, somewhere I felt Aarushi should not put herself into this mess, but it was impossible to convince her not to fight against injustice as she had been through hell thorough out her life.

It was midnight and Swati was getting ready to sleep, when Aarushi asked her about Divya. Swati was shocked to hear that. She could not speak a single word as she was wondering how Aarushi came to know about Divya incident.

"Who told you about Divya?" asked Swati, arranging pillows on the bed.

"Does it matter? I want to know what exactly happened with Divya? Did she commit suicide or was she murdered?" asked Aarushi helping Swati to make her bed. Swati looked at Aarushi for a while and then walked out to the balcony. Aarushi followed her as she wanted to know the reality.

"You can't turn your face from a situation like this," said Aarushi holding Swati's arm. Swati sighed and agreed to narrate the whole incidence. Whatever Swati said, was exactly the same as narrated by Salim.

"So, why didn't anyone take a step against it?" asked Aarushi.

"What do you want them to do? Go and log an FIR against Himanshu, then later go viral over internet and get a tag of whore overnight?" replied Swati in anger. Aarushi could understand the emotions Swati was going through. She hugged Swati tightly and said, "Do you think, not fighting against it is the best solution?"

"What do you mean? Tell me what should I do?" replied Swati loosening the grip.

"I know that there are a few more girls in the hostel who are victim of this scandal. All I want to say is they are not free. This hostel is nothing less than a prison to them. Himanshu can blackmail them anytime and use them as a sex toy whenever he wishes. Don't you think we should take a strong step against it?" said Aarushi in an attempt to convince Swati. After a few minutes of silence, Swati nodded her head to help Aarushi in her pursuit of justice.

"You are right. We can't simply sit with hands-on-hands. Let's fight and get that bastard behind the bars along with the bitch," said Swati hitting hard at the wall. Her anger was easily noticeable. She had this frustration from long and that day, because of Aarushi, she had gathered strength to fight against it.

"First, I need to know who are the other girls in this hostel who have been to Himanshu's party?" said Aarushi offering a stool to Swati.

"Ramya, Kajal and Preeti. They all stay in room number 102. The warden once took them to Himanshu's party saying Himanshu wants to assist them financially for their education if they clear the CAT exams. All three of them are preparing for CAT exams and work at a call centre in Rajender Nagar," said Swati. She was completely engrossed in her thought while she was narrating the story.

"It happened recently. I think, just a week before you joined. I remember, that night before going to the party, Ramya came to my room to borrow a sandal. She was dressed in a baby pink top and a faded pair of jeans. She looked really cute. I asked her where she was going, to which she replied that the warden was taking her, Kajal and Preeti, to a party. She looked quite excited," Swati said and then looked at Aarushi with teary eyes.

"They were raped, molested and photographed. When I asked them to log an FIR, they denied as they were warned by the warden that their video and photographs would get uploaded on the internet. To save themselves from insult, they chose to remain silent. Somewhere I too was afraid to raise a voice against it. But now, I am not," said Swati, wiping off her tears and offering support to Aarushi.

"Then let's plan our strategy to expose the warden and Himanshu. We need to talk and convince at least one among those three girls. Who do you think would be easy to convince?" asked Aarushi. Swati thought for a while and said, "Ramya."

"Great! Tomorrow, we are inviting Ramya to our room. I will try to find some excuse to get her to our room. Warden is anyway on vacation so we need not worry about her intervention," planned Aarushi. Swati, like a silent follower, nodded her head in acceptance.

"Hey, by the way Aaryan has asked me to say sorry to you on his behalf," said Aarushi while placing a kettle over the induction heater to prepare tea.

"Okay. It's good that he did or else I would have made his life hell," replied Swati. Aarushi smiled and asked Swati not to trouble him anymore.

"Oh ho, so madam is now having feelings for Aaryan. I can smell something fishy between you guys," taunted Swati, throwing a rose from the vase on Aarushi.

"Hey you idiot, don't throw it. I love roses," said Aarushi and kept the rose in between the pages of one among the hundreds of her thick books.

"Okay, so you love roses. Now see how this guy is going to get roses for you every day," said Swati with a crooked smile on her face. She picked her cell phone and messaged him.

"I can see that she is developing feelings for you inside her heart. It's perfect time to gift her rose. You have to do it daily without letting her know."

Nikhil and I were almost slept when the beep sound of the message woke me up. I was shocked to see the message from the lady astrologer at midnight. I rubbed my eyes to read the message. The first part of the message was a blessing to read, but the second part was challenging.

"From where the hell will I get roses?" I murmured. Nikhil was fast asleep when I slowly shook him to wake up. He jumped out of fear hoping something evil happened. I was sitting right in front of him when he asked, "*Kya hua* (what happened)? Why you did you wake me?" He looked everywhere in the room to assure that there was no fire. My heart wanted to ask about the "rose" issue, but my brain warned me not to. I remained silent which made Nikhil more furious on me.

"*Ab bolega kya hua?*" yelled Nikhil. Though it was dark, but I was able to visualize the anger in his eyes. I was expecting a slap any moment. I decided not to talk and sleep. I laid down and pulled the blanket to cover myself, while Nikhil was still wondering why he was awake.

"*Sale, harami* (You bastard), now you want to sleep. Why the hell did you wake me up?" shouted Nikhil, kicking my butt. I almost saved myself from falling down the bed.

"Where will I get roses in the colony?" I asked in a low tone, I silently kept my left leg on the floor to run in case of emergency. Nikhil was shocked to hear that question from me. He was trying to breathe heavily and calm down his anger.

"In the middle of the night, you woke me to ask where you will get roses in the colony?" repeated Nikhil.

"Yeah! Any idea," I replied and this time I had both my legs ready hanging on the floor to run. Nikhil looked at me for a while and then he did what I had already anticipated. He leaped on to me and the next moment we both were on the floor. Two punches on my stomach and six kicks on my butt were enough to bring his anger down.

"Sale, if you repeat this again, I swear on my mom, I will buy a rose garland to hang it over your framed picture," threatened Nikhil. I stood up and did some stretching to get rid of the pain. That night, to avoid anymore kicks, I decided to sleep on the sofa.

The next morning, as usual, I convinced myself to go to office. I searched for online websites for delivery of roses. This was the only productive thing I did the whole day in office. There were lots of websites offering the service. I wondered how many hungry souls of love we had in India that was making these websites run. I visited the one that was listed in the first page of Google.

"Rs 850 for a bouquet." I was shocked to see the price tag. Not willing to pay that much for a bunch of roses, I looked for some cheaper options. It was not that I was worried about money, but the worth of the product.

"Rs 70 for a single rose," I murmured. Nikhil looked at my screen to check what I was doing. After looking at roses on my screen, his face turned red. I looked at him and said, "What? You didn't help me, so I asked Google."

"You have not fixed a single bug since morning and you are looking for roses. You are screwed," whispered Nikhil, showing me his middle finger. I looked at him innocently and then said, "I have been bitten by love bug, and trust me it's not easy to fix it."

Nikhil smiled and asked me to carry on my stupidity. I selected the single rose option and went to the payment section.

"Service tax, delivery charge, VAT, total Rs 146.74," I whispered to myself while struggling to justify the total amount I was asked to pay.

"Nikhil, I think we should leave this headache job and start selling roses," I said. He sighed and then moved his chair back to look at me. I was trying to show him the price, but he looked least interested.

"The way you are working, I am quite confident that one day you will be selling roses on street. Don't worry, I will buy one daily," taunted Nikhil.

"*Stupid*, you are ready to buy that time. But now when I am asking for your help, you are behaving as if I am asking for your kidney," I responded.

"Don't drag me into your stupidity. Unlike you, I have work," said Nikhil and got engrossed with his codes.

I thought for a while to buy the rose or not, then I called Salim. I was confident he would help me out.

"Aaryan Bhaiya, what happened," said Salim as soon as he picked the call.

"What happened? Can't I call you at this time?" I asked.

"You can call me 24*7. You are a gem!" said Salim. I was quite shocked to hear that.

"Bhai, your 'Gem' needs a favour. I need a rose to give Aarushi. I searched online and it's quite expensive. Could you please arrange one? I will collect it from you at night," I demanded the favour. Salim was mute for a while and then replied, "Done."

"Great! I will pay you for that," I said.

"No need to pay. I am not buying it anyway. Our neighbour, Sharma Ji, has planted lots of roses in his garden. And most of the time, his house remains vacant. I will pluck one for you," replied Salim enthusiastically. Though, I didn't like the idea of trespassing Sharma Ji's private property, but I had no other choice.

"Make sure no one catches you," I suggested him.

"No need to worry at all. I am expert in hide and seek. You will get the rose by evening," confirmed Salim. After a few more discussions on bollywood superstar, Salman Khan's breakup, we ended the call.

Time passed and office hours were soon over. It was around 8:00 pm when Nikhil and I stepped inside our room. We were tired. Nikhil jumped on the bed without even removing his shoes.

"No matter what, don't wake me. I am tired, I need to sleep like a dead human," ordered Nikhil and buried under the blanket.

"What about dinner?" I asked changing my dress. Nikhil peeked out of the blanket and yelled, "Let me sleep. I don't want to eat. I want to sleep. Is that clear?"

"Yep!" I said putting the slippers on. Nikhil sighed and again covered himself with the blanket. I decided to collect the rose from Salim and take my dinner at his place itself. I slowly opened the door to avoid any noise. But before I decided to leave, the monster in me wanted to irritate Nikhil further.

"Bhai, Bhai, Bhai," I said to wake up Nikhil. Frustrated, he woke up asking, what?

"Where will I find roses?" I said and ran downstairs; two stair at a time. I could hear his slangs dedicated to all my blood relations.

"Hey Salim *Bhai,*" I greeted Salim. He was busy in tuning the radio to catch his favourite Bollywood songs channel.

"Are *Gulabo* (rose)!" taunted Salim. I really wanted to hit him hard to call me '*Gulabo*' in front of a few of his customers who were having their dinner. They all looked at me and laughed. I went closer to Salim and said, "Sale Kamine, 'Gulabo' kisko bola be? (You rascal, whom did you call 'Gulabo'?)"

"Oho, I am sorry, I was about to say *Gulaab* (rose), but 'Gulabo' came out," explained Salim. I calmed down myself and asked for the rose which Salim was supposed to get.

"Here it is. I jumped the fence and got it for you. There was no one at Sharma Ji's home," said Salim giving me the rose.

"Thanks. But why did you jump the fence if no one was there? You could have entered through the gate. I hope it was not locked," I asked him.

"The gate was not locked but jumping the fence has a thrill and adventure. Why to miss it?" replied Salim pointing at the picture of Salman Khan nailed at one of the walls. I smiled and thanked him again for taking the not-so-required risk of jumping a 3ft tall boundary.

"If the door is not locked and Salim got the rose, then why shouldn't I try to get one myself. Afterall, it's all done by Salim, and there wasn't any contribution from my end," my heart made me think.

Sharma Ji's house was just a minute walk from Salim's hotel. I reached there and was about to open the gate when Salim's statement striked my brain.

"Dude, there is no adventure unless you jump the boundary," I said to myself and a mere thought of this stupid adventure brought a crooked smile on my face, I was feeling as if I had to jump a cliff to get the rose. But, it's true that God is watching all of us everytime. God can fulfill our needs, but not greeds. I tried to jump over the boundary and landed badly on the other side. I fell over the rose garden and while balancing myself to avoid hitting my face on the ground, I scratched my hands and legs.

"Fuck you Sharma," I yelled in my conscience. Mr. Sharma had planted hell lot of rose plants and that too near the boundary wall. He should have at least considered that there were few adventurous guys in the colony.

I dusted myself, and quickly plucked one rose and came out of the house through the main gate. No more adventure.

I messaged Aarushi to ask if her warden was there in the hostel or not. After waiting at her hostel gate for almost ten minutes, I got her reply.

"No, she is on vacation. But why r u asking?" she messaged back.

I didn't reply anything as I wanted to surprise her. I wanted her to see the rose in my hand and feel the love in my heart. I rushed to her room and knocked the door.

"Who is there?" asked Swati. I could recognize her voice. I remained silent and knocked again. I could hear some low decibel discussions. I knocked again.

"Let me open the door," said Swati and unlocked the door. I was standing right in front of her with a flower in my hand and a stupid smile over my face.

"You! Why are you here?" yelled Swati. I was not expecting that kind of welcome. It hurt me a little, but then I saw Aarushi sitting at the corner of her bed, with her legs crossed and a cushion on her lap. Without giving a second thought, I entered the room and went straight to Aarushi's bed.

"Aarushi,

I have got this rose for you. I stole it from my neighbour's garden.

But the blood that you see coming out of my finger, is my own.

I have no idea why I did this? No idea, why you love roses?

All I know is, I love you and I love you. So, please say, do you love me?

Say or else, I will keep coming to you with roses, until you accept my love or I bleed to death plucking them."

Aarushi was speechless. She froze on her bed. Our eyes were locked with each other and honestly, I badly wanted to hug her. I could see her little cute smile and moist eyes. My heart was pounding quite fast and I could easily listen to my heartbeats. Swati too could not say anything and was standing right behind me waiting for an answer from Aarushi.

"*Didi* (elder sister), say yes" said someone hiding behind the balcony curtain. I removed the curtain to check. She was Ramya. She was asked to get behind the curtains when I knocked the door.

"Come out Ramya," said Swati. Ramya slowly stepped out of the curtain. She looked nervous. Aarushi asked her to grab a chair and relax. I too stood up and placed myself on Aarushi's bed. Though Aarushi was not comfortable with that as two other girls were watching us at that moment, but she didn't overreact. To make things normal, she placed a cushion between us to draw the line of control.

"Wait, I will come," said Aarushi and got up from her bed.

"Where are you going? Its fine, I can sit on a chair or even stand, but you don't leave," I said as I felt she was not comfortable having me on her bed.

"I am not leaving. And you don't need to grab a chair," said Aarushi peeling a garlic clove. Her reply though gratified my heart, shocked the other two girls in the room. Aarushi could not notice Swati and Ramya's facial reaction when they heard her approving my presence on her bed. Swati then gestured me a thumbs up to congratulate me for that little success.

"Show me where you have got bruises," asked Aarushi.

"The biggest one is in my heart. Shall I show you?" I replied gesturing to open my shirt. Ramya and Swati closed their eyes as they were expecting something romantic to happen between Aarushi and me. Aarushi was quite embarrassed and slapped me slowly on my cheek.

"Girls relax, he is an idiot," said Aarushi and rubbed the garlic clove over my bruises on forearm.

"Shit, it burns. Don't you have any antiseptic cream," I yelled out of pain.

"This is the best antibiotic. And moreover, you showcase yourself as very strong man. You should not complain about such little pains?" taunted Aarushi with a cunning smile on her face.

"Kuch is tarah usne humare zakhmo ko chhua,
Dil kiya pure jism ko cheer ke rakh du."

"Waah!" appreciated Swati. Ramya too clapped to recognize my talent. Though Aarushi just made a frustrated face and rubbed the garlic clove everywhere on my hands wherever she found a trace of blood.

After she was done practicing her Ayurvedic medical practice on me, she finally picked the rose and kept it inside one of her books.

"Thanks," said Aarushi tucking strands of hair her behind her ears.

"Okay, now tell me what's the plan? How are we going to expose Himanshu and your warden?" I asked unknown to the fact that Ramya was one of the victim.

Ramya looked at Swati and Aarushi in shock. Aarushi asked Ramya to relax, but Ramya didn't feel comfortable and she said, "Fine, you guys carry on, I have to go."

"Ramya wait. We need to talk to you," said Aarushi holding Ramya's hand to stop her from leaving. Ramya was not comfortable and she was unsure about the topic Aarushi wanted to discuss with her.

"What is that you want to talk?" asked Ramya sitting back on her chair.

Aarushi thought for a while and then said, "We know what happened with you. We want you to speak up. We want to help you. You can't live in this prison and pretend that everything is okay. You are a victim, not a criminal. You need to fight for justice Ramya," said Aarushi while holding Ramya's palms under hers. For Ramya, probably one of her worst secret was no more limited to herself. Now there were a few more who knew about that horrific incident. And someone was sitting right in front of her and demanding an answer from her.

What all did we really know about that incident? Would we ever understand her state of mind now and more importantly, how we came to know about the video, which was made when she was being molested along with her two other friends. Scores of such questions clouded Ramya's mind and she didn't have an answer to any for them.

Aarushi kept on insisting and tried to make her talk. But Ramya was lost in her fearful thoughts. She wondered who else knew about that incident. For a while, she thought her life has come to an end.

"Which incident are you referring to? I don't know Himanshu," murmured Ramya. Her face and body language didn't support her statement. In a state of panic she tried to get up from her chair, but Aarushi comforted and consoled her. Ramya remained quiet for a while and then suddenly she couldn't take it anymore and tried to rush out of the room. Aarushi jumped out of her bed and held her arms. Ramya's skin felt ice cold. She was shivering.

"I never took Himanshu's name," said Aarushi. Ramya's face turned red. She looked at Swati and said, "Didi, it must be you who shared our dark secret with everyone. Why did you do this? Don't you realize how tough it is for me and my other two roommates to live a life in this prison and act as if everything is normal," Ramya had tears in her eyes and she felt betrayed.

Before Swati could have explained everything to Ramya, Aarushi hugged Ramya tightly.

"Please let me help you, Ramya. You are like my little sister, I can't see you like this," pleaded Aaurshi. Perhaps it was the soothing sound of her voice or the warmth of her body that comforted Ramya. Ramya could not hold back her emotions any longer and she broke into tears. She cried her heart out. She gave voice to her emotions when she cried loudly. Aarushi allowed her to vent her feelings. She continued to hold her body close to her chest and in the tight grip of her arms. She kept rubbing her back gently, allowing her to lighten.

I stood up to offer a glass of water to Ramya. She looked at me and said, "Hope you don't share this with anyone."

"Not even at my last breath," I assured. Ramya took a sip of water and relaxed herself on the chair. Aarushi sat beside her to make her comfortable.

"What do you want to know? My life is now in the hands of the warden. She is a bitch. She was the one who was standing there and making videos when those monsters were molesting us. We cried for help, but she asked us to cooperate. I was asked to strip before Himanshu on a condition that I won't be raped. Fearing the physical torture one has to go after being raped, I unwillingly stripped every single cloth on my body whilst the bitch kept recording. I was begging to them, falling on their feet pleading for mercy, but nothing melted their hearts," narrated Ramya. Her eyes were red and even tears dried up. She looked lost in her dark memories.

"A few days after that incident, I went to the warden and asked her to delete the videos and let me leave the hostel. She laughed and showed me the video that she had kept in her computer and warned me that the day I leave the hostel, she will upload it on the internet," narrated Ramya.

"That means, if we get an access to her computer, we can erase all the videos," I put my point. All the ladies in the room looked at me as if I had suggested something nonsense.

"What? Why are you girls staring at me?" I said when no one appreciated my thought. Aarushi stood up and came near to me. I actually got scared.

"Don't slap me. Please. All these ideas are the result of watching Crime Patrol (a famous crime series)," I whispered innocently. Though I thought, no one else except Aarushi would have heard it, but I was wrong. All the three beautiful ladies in the room laughed out loudly. But this time, more than Aarushi's smile, it was Ramya's smiling face that pacified my heart.

"You are so sweet," said Aarushi while rubbing my cheeks. She didn't realize that Swati and Ramya too were witnessing her actions. I was anyway lost just by her touch. 'Sweet' was the word which was making encircling in my eyes. It was for the first time that a girl called me 'Sweet' instead of an 'Idiot'. Arushi soon realized what she did and to divert the topic from her she said, "Warden's room is locked. How will we be able to enter?"

"We can break the lock. It's a cakewalk for me," I

said with a pride smile on my face. It was not received well by the ladies though.

"Are you an experienced thief or a developer?" asked Swati while the other two ladies kept staring at me.

"How does it matter? Let's go and break it," I said with an excitement and looked forward for the same level of enthusiasm from the ladies, but they still had a doubt on my ability to break the lock.

"Fine. Anyway we don't have any other option than to trust him. Moreover, we are unsure about warden's arrival so we need to take this chance tonight," said Aarushi to convince the other two ladies. I was just waiting for them to nod their head, so that I could go ahead with the plan. Swati and Ramya looked at each other for an opinion, but having no other options they nodded their head and asked me to showcase the talent of breaking locks.

We grabbed a torch, a hammer, a small iron rod and a pen drive. I was leading the team of four. It was almost midnight and there was no one awake to witness our adventure. We walked slowly towards the warden's room.

"Light the torch," I ordered like a captain. Swati switched on the torch to show the lock. The warden was really a careless woman. She had locked her room with a chinese lock.

I sat to examine the lock as an FBI agent. I narrowed my eyes to look serious. All the ladies surrounded me and felt thrilled about the lock breaking ceremony. I asked Aarushi to sit beside me.

"What happened?" asked Aarushi with full curiosity. I made a serious face and said, "Take out your hair clip."

Wondering why was I asking her to do that, she followed my order and took out the clip. Her hair were now surfing her face and she looked beautiful under the bright moonlight.

I took her hair clip and kept it in my pocket. Aarushi looked at Swati to interpret why the hell did I ask her for the clip.

"Why did you ask for the clip?" asked Aarushi. I turned to her and said, "You look good when your hair just wave around your face. I love it when you tuck them behind your ears."

Swati and Ramya could not stop themselves from laughing. I too made an innocent face and smiled. Aarushi sighed and stood to avoid any more embarrassment.

"Okay, Ramya, you have got the hammer?" I asked Ramya.

"Yes," said Ramya and raised the hammer in air to show the ownership.

"Good," I said gesturing Ramya to calm down.

"Aarushi, have you got the iron rod?" I asked looking at Aarushi.

"Yes."

"Good," I continued, "Aarushi you place the rod underneath this latch and Ramya you slowly hit the hammer in the opposite direction, until I stop you," I said taking a step back and making space for the ladies to carry on the task.

"And may I know what role are you playing?" asked Swati, who was still standing there with the torch.

"I will guide you girls. I am the captain," I said confidently.

"Do you see this rod? I will hit you to death," said Aarushi showing the iron rod that she held in her hands. Getting scared, I took the rod from her and hammer from Ramya and got back to the job.

"You know Aarushi, if I would have said the same thing to Nikhil, that I was a Captain, he would have said,

'I will put this rod in your ass,' I said and laughed. I didn't realize that I had spoken a forbidden word in front of the ladies.

"Aarushi too meant the same though," a blunt reply came from Swati. I looked at Aarushi to confirm if Swati was correct. Aarushi denied Swati's claim by nodding her head to say no.

After fifteen minutes of hammering the latch, finally the latch came out. There was sense of relief on everyone of us. We entered inside and preferred not to switch on any lights.

Swati waved the torch at each and every corner of the room. I must say it was quiet clean and well arranged. A flower vase, a few photo frames, a split AC, a cot, a table with computer placed over it and a bookshelf. Though, our area of interest was the computer.

I switched on the computer and asked Swati to switch off the torch. The computer's light was bright enough for us to see each other.

"Hmm... its windows7," I said. All the ladies looked at me as if I had said something beyond their knowledge. I smiled and raised my collar to justify my computer science degree.

"It is locked," whispered Aarushi and looked at me. I dragged the chair and sat over it to have a closer look. Honestly, I just wanted to make them realize that I was the only brilliant computer geek in that room. They all gave me side while I placed myself on the chair.

"Girls, I have asked not to switch on the light, but at least you can switch on the fan," I was in full attitude. Swati gestured Ramya to obey my orders. Ramya did the needful.

"It's asking for the password," I murmured.

"Thanks for letting us know," taunted Ramya, "We can also read that."

"What are you waiting for? Crack it," ordered Aarushi. I realized the time had come to lower down my collar and politely leave the chair as I hardly knew anything about cracking the password, or for that matter, anything except JAVA language.

"Hmm... but it's unethical to hack someone's computer," I replied to hide my inability to crack the password, whilst I put my collar down. Ladies didn't get what I said. They were looking at me with a shock on their face.

"Was breaking the lock ethical?" asked Swati placing her hands on her waist.

"No, that was an adventure. You know as a computer science engineer, we take an oath during our final year of engineering, that no matter what the circumstances are, we would never hack someone's computer or any social network accounts someone owns," I replied in a single breath. I looked at their faces to check if anyone among them had agreed to my lie.

"Aaryan, look at me," said Aarushi. My heart pounded heavily while I turned to look at Aarushi.

"Now say the truth," she asked.

"I don't know how to crack the password. I am an engineer by degree, not by knowledge. I think we need to call Nikhil," I blabbered everything which I was trying to hide all this time. Aarushi smiled and said, "I knew it. I was just checking if you remember your promise which you made to me that you will be honest this time in your SSB interview."

I was actually feeling ashamed of myself. Without making my life more miserable inside that room, I called Nikhil. After a few rings he picked up the call.

"*Teri Ma ka, sale, harami,... (You bastard),*" yelled Nikhil over the phone. I would not have felt embarrassed if the phone would not have been in loudspeaker mode.

"*Bhai bas kar.* I am with Aarushi," I stopped Nikhil from creating any more scene over the phone.

"What the hell are you doing with Aarushi at this time?" asked Nikhil.

"I will tell you everything, but please be kind as the phone is on loudspeaker mode," I requested.

"Hey Nikhil, this is Aarushi. I need a help," said Aarushi over the speaker.

"Hi Aarushi. What happened?" asked Nikhil in a very soft tone. The monster who was yelling on me a few seconds before, was now behaving like a saint. He was such a rascal.

"We are inside warden's room and we need your help in cracking the password of her computer," explained Aarushi.

"How did you enter her room?" asked Nikhil. He sounded scandalized.

"*Tere bhai ne lock tod diya* (your brother broke the lock)," I said with a pride smile on my face. I looked at the ladies inside the room for an appreciation, but all of them gave a frustrated look to me.

"Yes, he broke the lock and he doesn't know how to break the password," taunted Aarushi. Nikhil was even more rude as he laughed loudly after hearing that.

"You have called Nikhil to ask for help or to do my insult," I sighed.

"Fine. I am coming. Just give me a second," said Nikhil and hung up the call.

"Huh, Computer engineer; Ethics; Windows7," were a few of the taunts which I received in the dark while we were waiting for Nikhil to arrive. I was just sitting quiet until Ramya asked Aarushi if the latter was sure about her choice.

"What do you mean by choice?" I asked lightening the torch on Ramya's face. She covered her face and yelled at me to stop it.

"Because I feel that Aarushi *didi* likes you. And that's why I was asking her if she was sure about it," replied Ramya. She was too blunt. I looked at Aarushi as she was the best person to answer Ramya's ridiculous question. Anyway, I was happy that Ramya too felt Aarushi's soft corner for me.

"I don't know. But I am sure if Aaryan would not have been here with us tonight, it would have been tough for me to convince you girls and quite tough to trespass warden's premises," replied Aarushi.

She maintained a soft tone and kept looking at me while answering Ramya's question on her choice. It is tough for me to describe my feelings in words. I wished God had made Ramya and Swati blind for a minute, so that I could hug my love tightly onto my chest and kiss her passionately on her pink lips. I controlled myself and whispered, "Thanks" to Aarushi.

Knock, Knock...

"Great, Nikhil is here," said Aarushi and walked towards the door to unlock. I jumped to stop her from doing so.

"What happened?" asked Aarushi seeing my idiotic behavior.

"Wait, let me open it," I said and asked her to step back. Frustrated, she stepped back and gestured me to continue my insanity.

"Who is that?" I asked. I too knew the person standing behind the door was none other than Nikhil, but I was just trying to have fun by making him stand outside the door. But my happiness didn't last for long.

"I am the original computer science engineer. Also, the roommate of the fake one who is inside," replied Nikhil.

I really wanted to open the door and choke him to death. What really annoyed me was the happiness and joyfulness on Swati's face. She was rolling over floor laughing at my miserable condition.

"You intentionally get yourself insulted," said Aarushi and asked me to get aside while she opened the door for Nikhil. The computer geek entered with a big smile on his face. Due to the darkness inside the room, he was unable to see our faces. He narrowed down his eyes to locate me in the dark.

"Hey, what are you doing in front of the computer? That's not your baby," said Nikhil after he found me sitting in front of the computer. I left the chair for him and asked him to place his ass over it.

Nikhil started performing some actions on the keyboard and within ten minutes he was able to unlock the computer. While he was occupied in hitting the keys, all the ladies in the room surrounded Nikhil to witness the magic. I simply laid over the bed and preferred to remain silent for my own goodness.

"Excellent!" praised Swati and looked at me with a frown face. I didn't react as there was no point in defending myself.

"Now we need to search the location where she might have kept the videos," suggested Aaurshi. I too joined them while Nikhil was opening each and every folder present on the drive.

"Shall I suggest something?" I interrupted. Though, Swati was not at all in a mood to listen to me, but I got Ramya's and Aarushi's approval to present my suggestion.

"Guys, all we want is to expose your warden and Himanshu. I don't think we should be using video related to any girl who still lives in the hostel. It may endanger their security," I put a genuine concern. Everyone looked at me with a dubious expression.

"See, what I am trying to say is, why not fight for Divya instead of any other girl," I continued. "Divya is no more and hence, Himanshu or even your warden can't blackmail her to step back."

"Wow! This is a great idea Aaryan," said Aarushi looking into my eyes. I was still unsure if she was serious or she was going to make fun of me. But later, even Ramya and Swati appreciated me for the suggestion. Ramya looked satisfied and happy that I didn't take her name in front of Nikhil.

"You may not be the best computer science engineer, but you are the best soul," commented Ramya as she realized my efforts to keep her name secret. Aarushi smiled and blinked her eyes to show how much she appreciated my thoughtful approach.

"Guys, see here," said Nikhil opening a folder that was named 'Hostel_Highlights'. There were many video files inside that folder. I was afraid that Ramya would feel uncomfortable if any of those videos were played. I pinched Nikhil and gestured him to not open any file.

"Okay, now just copy all the videos to your pen drive and once copied, don't forget to delete all the videos from the system," said Nikhil leaving the chair and getting aside. Nikhil and I sat on the cot to give Aarushi and other two girls a comfortable space. Aarushi copied all the videos from the computer and later deleted them. Now we had a proof with us to expose the warden and Himanshu. We all could see the happiness and satisfaction on Ramya's face. She was no more afraid of the warden. She was now free to leave the hostel premises any time she wanted without fear of blackmail.

Aarushi copied all the videos to her pen drive and then deleted them from the warden's system. It was almost

3:30 am when we were done with our task.

"Aaryan, Nikhil, thank you so much for your help," said Aarushi and extended her hand for a handshake. Before Nikhil could have responded, I quickly grabbed her hand and completed the handshake. Nikhil laughed and said, "You are such an idiot. I am not running away with her," Aarushi too smiled and said, "Aaryan, my palms are paining now. Could you please leave them now?" I realized that I was pressing Aarushi's palm for a while. I left the grip and set her free.

"Shall we go?" asked Nikhil looking at me. It was tough for me to say yes. I wanted some more time with Aarushi. But before I could have voiced my opinion, Aarushi too realized that it was too late and we all should go back to our respective rooms.

"You guys carry on. I will stay here for a while," I said gesturing everyone except Aarushi to leave. Swati and Ramya smiled as they could sense my desire to have a private time with Aarushi. They wished good night and left to their rooms. Nikhil too left from the scene patting on my back with a cunning smile on his face. Now it was just I and my love standing there under the blanket of clear sky.

Aarushi looked at me with a smile on her face and asked, "So, what's next?" I was speechless as I had nothing to talk. I just wanted to be there with her and spend a little more time admiring her.

"Nothing as such. Just that my heart was not satisfied. It wanted to have a few more moments with you," I whispered looking into her eyes. I badly wanted to hug her. She looked beautiful. Aarushi sighed.

"I am leaving tomorrow for the interview. I don't know how I will be able to live for the next five days without having a glimpse of you. You are not my habit, but need of my life. I was never like this. I never thought a day would come when my happiness would depend upon someone else. I miss you every moment. People say no addiction is good. But loving you is that addiction which if I quit, I will die. I don't know what destiny has planned for me and neither do I care about it, you know why?" I said taking a step closer to Aarushi and looking deep into her eyes. Aarushi stood froze.

"Because unlike you, I don't have a choice. You can either opt to leave me or love me, but I just know that the day my eyes won't see you would be the day my eyes will get closed forever," I said. My eyes were moist and so were hers. I knew, she wanted to express her feelings, but she was stopping herself from falling into any commitments. I could understand how tough it would be for a girl to fall in love who had already been through a racking past.

Taking a deep breath to control her emotions, she looked into my eyes and said, "Aaryan, please never ever think that I have a choice to leave you. I know how I feel when I am with you. If I didn't have feelings for you, I would have left along with Swati and Ramya, but I wanted to stay with you. It was not just your heart, which was not satisfied, it was mine too which was pinching me to hold your hand and stop you from going. I don't know what stops me from accepting you love. Why is it so tough for me to express my feelings? Everyone who loved me left me all alone at the early stage of my life. It required enough strength to come out of it and live a normal life. Your love for me makes me scared. I don't know if I would ever be able to survive if you leave me one day. I don't have enough strength left to overcome another loss. Sometimes I feel, love is not meant for me. I am not born to be loved. But then when I see you, I feel I am special. I am special at least for someone. Thank you so much for making me realize that I am not an orphan. You are there with me. And the day, I gather enough strength to voice my feelings for you I will be the one, who would be running behind you madly and loving you more than anyone else. Trust me, ours will be the most passionate love the world would have ever seen," said Aarushi taking a step closer to me. There was hardly any gap between our chests. I could feel her heartbeat and her warm breath. Our noses were touching each other with every breath we took. Her soft pink-glossy lips were shivering and waiting to be kissed. My heart was pounding faster than ever. I badly wanted to grab my darling in my arms and kiss her until my last breath. Our body turned cold and I froze.

"What are you waiting for? I am not drunk today," said Aarushi. Her eyes were closed and lips opened to welcome mine. I brought my lips closer to hers and was all set for our first passionate kiss. As I was about to kiss her, a thousand butterflies stretched their wings and fluttered erratically in my stomach. *Why am I so nervous?* I knew it was because, I had no idea what kind of mood Aarushi was going to be in after our kiss was over. My inner goddess asked me not to worry about future troubles, but to live the present. I leaned forward and the moment our lips were about to meet, Aarushi pushed herself back and said, "Times up."

"What? This is wrong. I was about to kiss you," I said like a loser. Aarushi laughed and said, "You took a lot of time to decide. So, better luck next time."

I wanted to slap myself for missing this wonderful opportunity to experience our first kiss. Aarushi quickly hugged me and before I could have even realized and felt the warmth of her hug she ran towards the stairs wishing me good night.

"Come on. At least allow me to hug you," I yelled. Aarushi stopped at the stairs and turned back to look at me.

"You don't need my permission to hug me. But now the time is over. So, once you are back from Mysore, you can fulfil all your wishes," said Aarushi and winked. I too smiled and gave her a flying kiss. She grabbed my kiss in her palm and placed it on her chest. The best of her smile was on her face.

She looked extremely blissful and so was I. I was unable to understand what was happening. It was definitely a miracle. I could feel Aarushi's love for me. She hugged me, and if I would not have thought like a moron, we could have even had our first passionate kiss. Though it was strange, but a wonderful feeling was there in my heart. I wanted to shout, jump with joy, and dance like insane. Really, you feel good when you love someone, but you feel blessed and great, when that someone loves you back.

Chapter 16
And she said, "I love you"

* * *

The day came when I had to leave for Mysore and give my best at the interview. I was nervous about my selection but at the same time, I was feeling blissful as I had Aarushi in my life. Nikhil had left for office wishing me all the best and assuring me that he would take care of Aarushi in my absence. I had to catch the flight at 2:30 pm to Bangalore and then catch a bus to Air Force Selection board in Mysore. I had to hurry up as it was almost quarter to 11, and I was still in bed. I first packed all the required stuffs and documents in a backpack. Then I took a quick bath and offered my prayer to *Hanuman Ji*, the only God idol in our room.

"Please make sure, Aarushi is safe in my absence. And also, be with her when she writes her IAS exam day after tomorrow. Make sure she clears it," I said to Lord Hanuman. I had nothing to ask for myself as now I had Aarushi, the best I could have ever asked for.

I quickly dressed up and booked a cab for the airport drop.

"Should I call her? She might be busy in her preparations, should I just go to her room and meet her once and million other questions were striking my brain while I was standing at the balcony waiting for the cab to arrive. I wanted to meet Aarushi, but I was not sure if she would feel comfortable having me in her room.

"She should not think that I am taking her hug and her positive reaction about my flying kiss as a signal to approach her," I talked to myself. I killed the idea of going to her room, within my heart, and decided to just call her and wish her luck for her exams.

Knock Knock... I heard someone knocking at the door. I went to open the door.

"Aarushi," I said in a surprise. She looked at me with a pleasant smile on her face and asked my permission to enter. I gave her way to enter the room. I was still standing at the door looking at her when she asked me to stop staring and close the door.

"Are you here to complete the kiss that could not happen last night?" I asked sounding naughty. She came closer to me and said, "I am here to make sure Flight Lt Aaryan Rathod gets all the blessings before he leaves for the interview."

I gathered some inner strength and walked a little closer to her. Aarushi neither moved nor felt awkward. She still had the smile on her face, which boosted my confidence, and I grabbed her waist round my arms and pulled her closer to my chest. I was quite unsure about her reaction, but she was just watching me getting closer and closer to her.

"What next?" asked Aarushi sounding little nervous. She was in my arms breathing heavily and the gap between our lips was in millimetres. Her waist was so soft and curvy that it was almost impossible to convince myself take my hands off from them.

"Nothing. Just look at your eyes, and kiss you at the best available opportunity," I said smiling. Aarushi too smiled and took out a bowl which she was hiding under her dupatta.

"What is it?" I asked letting her free from the grip. She had brought sweet curd for me. In India, it is called a superstition that eating sweet curd before exams brings good luck.

"Can you get me a spoon?" asked Aarushi.

"You are preparing for IAS, and you believe in all these superstitions. I can't believe it," I said surprisingly. Aarushi ignored my comment and asked me to get a spoon.

"If eating curd would have brought good luck in exams, then I would have topped in IIT exams and for that matter any other exams which I attempted and failed," I taunted.

Aarushi could not take it anymore and she took a little portion of curd in her hand and asked me to open my mouth. A shiver went through my body as I never expected her to feed me with her hands. I opened my mouth to eat the sweet curd from the hands of the sweetest person on the Earth. Aarushi fed me the curd and while doing so, our eyes were locked into each other and everything else came to a standstill. There was a romantic vibe in the room.

"Wait," I said when Aarushi took her hands off after feeding me.

"What?" asked Aarushi wondering why I asked her to wait. I went closer to her and held her hands which still had a little trace of curd left on her fingers. I licked each of her fingers while she stood frozen and could not stop me from doing so. There was such a silence in the room that we could hear our heartbeats. Soon after coming to senses,

Aarushi blushed and took a step back wiping her fingers with the dupatta.

"What happened?" I asked.

"Nothing," said Aarushi. She was still unable to control her breath. She was definitely thinking about something else. I wanted to make her comfortable, so I placed her on the sofa while I sat on the floor holding her hands between mine.

"Aaryan. I try to look strong, but trust me I fall weak whenever we get closer to each other. Promise me that you will never leave me alone. I can't handle any more pain," said Aarushi with heavy voice and moist eyes. I too could not control myself from shedding tears.

I kissed her forehead and said, "I promise you. I promise that I will never leave you alone. Not even in the scariest of dreams. I promise, either I will live with you the rest of my life, or I won't live at all."

Aarushi pulled my cheek and said thanks. Before we could have talked any further, I received a call from the cab driver.

"I need to go now," I said looking at Aarushi's eyes. She wiped her tears and stood up. I could notice that she was not comfortable and was trying to hide her emotions behind a fake smile.

"What happened? You don't seem to be happy. Don't you want me to go?" I asked. She looked everywhere else other than my eyes. I held her arms and asked her to look into my eyes. Her eyes were moist and she looked confused.

"I don't know Aaryan. I had a very bad dream last night. I feel I won't be able to see you anymore. Till now I was just trying to ignore everything and spend a good time with you. But now when you are leaving, I can't hide my emotions any more. I don't know what I am doing. I know this is stupid, but somewhere I am not comfortable. I can't afford to lose you," cried Aarushi. I was shocked to hear that. *How can such a strong girl be so emotional?*

"Aarushi, please don't cry. It was just a bad dream. I promise you, I will come back. And moreover I am just going for an interview not for a war," I said giving a tight hug to my sweetheart. She looked at me with her teary eyes and smiled saying, "The day you will be going for war, I would be stronger than you could ever imagine,"

"Shall I ask you one thing?" I asked. Aarushi wiped her tears and looked at me.

"I know you love me. But I still don't know, why don't you say it? Just once, say that you love me," I requested.

Aarushi smiled and said, "I don't want you to be distracted during your interview. Go, clear your exams, and the day you arrive, you will have your wish fulfilled."

I took that as a promise from her. Aarushi accompanied me to the cab. We were holding hands until we reached near the cab. I didn't feel bad when Aarushi stole her hands out of my grip when we reached downstairs as she didn't want anyone to make any wrong assumptions.

I sat inside the cab, and wished her all the best for her exams. She thanked me and wished me a successful and safe journey. Half of my heart was feeling sad as I won't be able to see her for another five days, but the other half was excited to conquer the SSB interview.

For me, Air Force was a dream, but for her, IAS was a reason to live. Aarushi used to say, *"If you have a dream but no action plan, then you are simply passing your time."*

After 2 hours of flight from Delhi to Bangalore and another 6 hours in the bus to Mysore, I reached the venue where all the candidates were asked to assemble. Like me, there were thirty others who were waiting there for a pickup. We were told to wait for the Air Force bus which was scheduled to pick us from the venue at 5:30 am. Waiting at the venue for almost 2 hours, and smoking almost a packet of cigarette, I was able to make a few good friends. Saurabh Sharma, and Shakti were the ones just like me. They both wanted to get rid of the corporate world and live a life with honour and dignity. It was around 5:30 am when we saw a light blue bus with Air Force emblem at its both sides stopped near us. A gentleman in Air Force uniform, asked us to show our admit card, and board the bus. As I have always been a back bencher, I quickly boarded the bus and acquired the last seat. Along with me sat, Saurabh and Shakti.

It took us another 30 minutes to enter the Air Force Selection board. The moment we entered the portals of the selection centre we felt the essence and the atmosphere of defence bases in India. Even in the heart of the city of Mysore, Air Force never compromises with the ecological balance they have in their bases, lots of greenery around. There was a discipline. It was nothing less than a temple, where as soon as you enter the decibels of your sound reduces drastically. And the only time you are allowed to create noise is when you are doing your ground tests.

All candidates were asked to complete the document verification process. Thereafter, we went through a psychological test and a group discussion. After the test we were allotted chest numbers. That was a sort of an ID card and we all were supposed to interact with our fellow batch mates by referring them either as gentleman or by their chest number. My chest number was 41.

It was a wonderful feeling to look at the crowd and realize that there exist so many souls who take pride serving the nation instead of working for IT companies. But along with all good points, there was a bad one too. We were not allowed to use smart phones in the campus. There was a

PCO through which candidates could make a call during their free time.

I, along with several other aspiring officers, was allotted a bed in the barrack. It was an amazing experience. There were around thirty beds in the barrack. Table fans were provided for the beds which were out of reach from the ceiling fan.

The whole day was spent in writing several tests. It was a bit tiresome for all. At night, after the dinner I went to the PCO to call Aarushi. The PCO was located near the cafeteria and it was always monitored by a staff.

"Sir, I need to make a call," I took permission from the guard who was busy in maintaining some records. He looked at me and asked my name. Thereafter he noted my chest number and permitted me to dial the number. The phone was kept on a table and there was no privacy. I felt quite uncomfortable as the guard didn't go out of the PCO to allow me some space.

I picked up the receiver and dialed Aarushi's number. Before my first ring could have ended, she picked the call.

"Were you sitting over the phone?" I asked laughing.

"I was waiting for your call. How was your first day today," asked Aarushi. She was more enthusiastic than me.

"Aah… it was quite a tiring day. Filling forms, writing tests and moreover following a disciplined life," I said without realizing that the guard too was listening to my statements. I looked at him and smiled to lighter the moment, but his facial expression didn't change. He looked serious and furious on me. Perhaps the discipline word didn't go well with him.

"Actually I am loving it here. People are so nice and the food quality is awesome. I wish I stay here forever," I lied intentionally to make the guard feel comfortable. But then,

Aarushi was not comfortable with my statements.

"So you don't want to come back. Have you found any beautiful girl in the campus or what? Good for you," replied Aarushi. Girls will be girls!

"No, it's not like that. Please, you know what I meant. Anyway, how is your preparation going?" I asked. I was cursing the guard who was continuously looking at me and because of that I was talking silly stuffs with Aarushi.

"Since when did you start behaving so serious? You never asked me about my preparations. Let me guess, is there someone sitting beside you?" asked Aarushi. I got a smile on my face when she guessed my pathetic situation.

"Yeah you are right," I said with a smile on my face and looking into the eyes of the guard. Aarushi laughed out loud and started teasing me.

"Come on Aaryan, say one shayari for me. Come on. I want to listen one,"

"Huuuh… so what time is your exam tomorrow?" I asked ignoring her demand for shayari.

"Okk, I won't force you now. I can understand your pity situation. I will be leaving tomorrow at 11:00 am," replied Aarushi.

"Okay. All the best, and I am 100 per cent sure, you will make it through," I said. I was sounding like a moron. I had never talked to her like this before.

"Thanks. And I am sure, this time you will make it through. Chalo, now you keep the phone and go to sleep. You have to follow a disciplined life after all," she said.

"Yeah, I am practicing it now itself," I said and after a few more formal talks we hung up the call. I went to the guard and asked how much I needed to pay.

"Rs 35," said the guard noting the amount in the register. I took out the money from my wallet and gave it to him. Initially, I thought of talking to him for a while, but later dropped the idea as I was scared he would push me out of the PCO. Yes, he was not at all in a great mood.

"Thank you Sir," I said and was about to step out when the guard stopped me. I turned back to listen him.

"I know the food is not great. But it is equally true that you are here for an interview and not for vacation," said the guard. I smiled and said, "True". Thereafter, he got engrossed with his register and I left to the barrack with a hope of a wonderful tomorrow.

Next day was quite a tiring day, as it required us to perform some ground tasks. Monkey crawling, jumping 8ft wall, snake race, rope climbing to name few. After a tiring day and a depressing dinner, I again went to PCO. Aarushi had her exams in the morning and I knew she would be waiting for my call.

"Aaryan Rathod, chest number 41," I said to the guard while taking the stool to sit. He looked at me and smiled. I was shocked to know that he could actually smile. I felt quiet relaxed after his smile.

"Don't worry. I am sitting outside. Talk freely. And don't forget to dedicate a shayri to her today," said the guard and stepped out of the PCO. He placed himself on a bench which was kept outside the PCO. I thanked him for his gesture, but I was equally surprised to know that he actually heard my last call.

I dialed the number and waited for Aarushi to pick the call. The ring was over but she didn't pick my call. I got worried and dialed again.

"Hello Aaryan," said Aarushi. She was breathing heavily.

"Hi. What happened? Sounds like you have been running," I said

"Yeah I was on the terrace when you called me. Sorry, I could not pick that first time as Swati had snatched my cellphone to tease me. So finally when she felt pity on me, she handed it back," justified Aarushi.

I loved to hear that she was teased by her friends by my name. It's a kind of great achievement in any aspiring lover's resume.

"So what was she saying?" I tried to drill further.

"Nothing. Simply that *oye hoye.. Aa haaa...* You know that girly talks," she laughed.

"Good to hear that. Anyway, how was your exam?" I asked.

"It was great. I am 100 per cent sure that I would clear it. And I was celebrating a pre-success party at the terrace," she said out of excitement.

"Great! I too know that you would make it through. By the way, were you girls boozing?" I asked sounding curious.

"Yeah. Coke and Sprite," she chuckled.

"What? Are you drinking them neat?" I was worried as I hardly remember when was the last time that I and Nikhil had tasted Coke. We always mixed Old Monk, the best rum, with Coke.

"Yes. We are having Coke on the rocks," taunted Aarushi.

"Hey Aaryan, I wanted to tell you something," said Aarushi. She sounded quiet serious which made me tensed.

"What is it?" I asked.

"I am not sure about Warden's arrival. And moreover, we didn't repair her room's lock, so she can easily find out of the mischief happened," she said.

"I am planning to log the FIR tomorrow. I can't wait for the warden to come. She might get all of us in trouble," explained Aarushi. I was not happy with her idea and suggested her to wait until I arrived there. But, she was not ready to risk my career.

"I don't want you to be involved in this. She might blame you for the theft which I don't want. I can handle it. You just concentrate on you exams, and come soon," said Aarushi ignoring my suggestion.

"Okay, if you think you really don't need me in this, then I am fine. You do whatever you want," I said as I was hurt with her behaviour. Aarushi could judge my feelings and she tried to pacify me.

"Please Aaryan, don't say this. You have already done a lot. And now when you are there to chase your dream, I can't risk it. The warden can't log an FIR against me as I am having all the videos, but she can log a complaint against you for breaking into her room and supporting the crime. I don't want that to happen. Please, don't take me wrong. I need you, always and forever," said Aarushi.

Though I understood the point she was trying to make, but I was not happy to let her walk alone in this journey. I was really surprised to know how much she cared for me and my dreams. She knew that somewhere she was endangering her career, but she kept my dreams before hers. She was ready to pay the cost of love.

"Okay. But be carefull. I will call you tomorrow," I said. I was still unable to get normal and talk to her.

"Are you angry with me?" she asked. I could guess that she would have made a puppy face while asking that question.

"No I am not. Just worried," I replied.

"Okay, if you are not angry then before we hung up the call you have to say a shayari for me. I hope no one is sitting next to you," demanded Aarushi. I sighed. I was not in a great mood but somewhere I was happy to realize that, she cared for me and my dreams.

"Mujhse is qadar ishq kar ke
Tune na jaane kitne dil tode honge

Afsos to un sitaro par hota hai
Jo tere dua poori karne ko, asmaan se tuute honge."

"Waah… you made my day!" appreciated Aarushi. I again tried to convince her to not log a complaint until my arrival, but she politely declined my suggestion and asked me to concentrate on my interview.

"Okay, now you go to sleep. I need to go to the terrace or else girls will kill me," said Aarushi. I let her go as she wanted to enjoy that moment. But that night, I could not sleep. I was worried about Aarushi's safety. For a moment, I even thought of leaving the interview and fly back to Delhi but I knew, Aarushi would have hated me if I would have done that.

Next day, it rained heavily in Mysore. But nothing can stop defence personals as they didn't change the interview plan. We had to do our ground tasks in rain. It was quite tough to maintain balance on a plank of wood and the toughest was to climb a rope. But somehow, I did all that was asked.

Thereafter, I had a personal interview and two group discussions. Though I gave my best, but somehow I was not happy. Aarushi's safety was a concern for me.

Rain was not ready to call off for the day. It was around 9:30 pm when finally I decided to walk to the PCO to call Aarushi. I borrowed a plastic bag from Saurabh to cover my head. Though he asked me to wait for the rain to get over, but I denied as I knew what I was going through at that moment. I ran to the PCO. To screw my day further, the PCO was closed. I looked around for the guard, but he was nowhere. There was a notice board beside the PCO, which I had never bothered to read before. The time slot to place the call from that PCO was clearly mentioned over it. *"8:00 AM - 9:00 PM"*. I cursed myself to wait for an hour after the dinner in a hope that rain would get over. Helpless and drenched in rain, I walked back to the barrack for a sleepless night.

The final day arrived. The tension was clearly visible on each and every face. We had quite a lazy start to the day as we were supposed to report at 07: 00 am. Everyone had mixed feelings and hopeful thoughts. We had done what we could. We packed all our stuffs in our bags and wonderful memories in our hearts; and walked towards the conference hall.

Conference started by 10 am. All were seated in the same hall where we had the screening process. It was our last interview. Each candidate was called one-by-one inside a big conference room were almost twenty officers were sitting around an oval table. The best part was all the officers were in their uniform with shining badges on their chest. I, too, walked the red carpet and sat over the sofa which was placed at the center of the oval table. Before I could have got an opportunity to look around at officers, the Wing Commander, who took my personal interview, started asking me questions.

"Good Morning Aaryan," greeted the Wing Commander.

"Good Morning Sir," I greeted back.

"What do you think about the tasks you performed here?" he questioned.

"Sir, all the tasks especially the ground tasks were amazing. As a civilian I believe, I could have never got an opportunity to live these moments," I answered.

"Which task did you love the most and why?" upon came the next shot.

"I liked the group task. The reason being, during that task, I realised how important is team effort. I did not compete with anyone, but I just wanted my teammates to succeed. And the best part was, everyone else in the team, wanted the same."

"Do you know, where is the Air force training academy?" This came as a bouncer for me. I never really cared to know where it was. The only place that came in my tiny brain was Dehradun.

"Sir Dehradun," I replied without taking too much time. There was a deep silence in the room and within a few seconds, all the officers laughed.

"In Dehradun, we have the Indian Military Academy. You don't even know where you would go for training, if selected?" asked the Wing Commander. I felt really embarrassed. But then, I remembered what Aarushi told me to be. She wanted me to be honest.

"Sorry Sir, I don't know. But I know one thing, no matter where the training academy is located, I will be there on my joining date," I replied with full confidence on my face and voice. The Wing Commander looked at me and smiled. Later, he wished me luck and asked me to wait at the conference hall for the result.

After everyone's interview was completed, the technical officer of the board came and announced the chest numbers of the candidates which were selected.

"Gentleman, first of all, let me congratulate all you for making up to this stage. Some of you or may be all get rejected today. We can compromise with quantity, but not with quality. But, this is not the end. You may not be fit today, but you may improve on your weaknesses and appear again for the exams. I will now announce the chest numbers of those candidates who are selected. Once you hear your chest number, come and stand over the podium," said the officer. I kept my fingers crossed.

"Chest number 23" announced the officer and we all looked around to find that lucky guy. He was Adhvik. We didn't have much communication, but he indeed was a good candidate. We all clapped for his selection.

"34". This lucky guy was none other than Saurabh. I was really happy for him. Saurabh stood and hugged me and Shakti. While leaving for the podium, he wished both us good luck.

"41" I was blank after hearing my number and couldn't respond to the officer aptly. I knew I had heard about this number before, but could not realize that I have been living with this number, over my chest, for the past five days. I was blank and came to my senses only when Shakti shook me awake. While walking towards the podium, I could see myself in Air Force uniform, with Ray Ban glasses over my eyes. Though, there were three men standing over the podium, but I felt as if Aarushi was jumping over the podium and celebrating my success.

"The last one is the chest number 53" announced the officer. Saurabh and I hugged each other to hear that chest number. That chest number belonged to none other than Shakti. Yes, we all three friends were selected in the Indian Air Force. Shakti came running and all three of us hugged each other. It was a day, which I can never forget. I will cherish those memories forever. But, for me forever is just a few hours more.

We stayed back for further filling up the forms and headed to the barracks of the recommended candidates. We were asked to appear for medical tests after five days. I was happy that now I could go back home and see Aarushi. More than that, what excited me most was Aarushi's promise that she would say, *'I love you'* to me. I could not wait more to hear those three wonderful words.

After completing all the formalities, Saurabh, Shakti and I hugged each other once again and planned to have fun when three of us would meet again during the medical exams. We were given our cell phones and now we were free to call anywhere we wished to inform the good news. I called Aarushi.

"Hey where the hell were you yesterday?" yelled Aarushi as soon as she picked up the call.

"Yesterday, it was raining heavily here. And by the time I reached the PCO it was closed," I explained.

"I was worried for you Idiot," said Aarushi. I felt she was crying.

"Are you crying," I asked

"No," said Aarushi. She sounded like a two years old baby.

"Oh my God. Were you so worried about me?" I asked her.

"Just shut up. By the way, you are coming today, right?" asked Aarushi wiping her tears.

"Yes. I will be there kissing you by 9:30 at night," I said sounding confident. Aarushi could not say anything, perhaps she was feeling shy.

"Okay. I have planned a surprise for you," said Aarushi.

"Great! I will wait for it. By the way don't you want to ask about my result," I asked as I was desperate to share the good news with her.

"Did you get your results? I thought it would take time for the results to be out. What happened tell me? I am excited," she sounded happy.

"Soon, I will be an officer in the Indian Air Force," I said with pride. There was silence for a couple of seconds, as Aarushi could not believe what she heard.

"Really?" asked Aarushi.

"What do you mean by really? You thought I would not get selected? Am I such an idiot?" I asked feeling offended by her 'really'.

"That's a great news Aaryan. Oh my God, I can't believe this. Aaryan do you realize that you have achieved your dream?" said Aarushi. She sounded more excited than me. It really feels great when someone feels more happiness for your achievement than you feel for yourself.

"My dream is still incomplete as I want stars on my shoulders and you by my side, forever," I told her.

"This is not just your dream. It's mine too," said Aarushi.

"Thank you so much Aarushi for being with me. I can't wait anymore to have you in my arms," I said.

"Me too. Hey don't you want to know what happened yesterday when I went to log the FIR against Himanshu and the warden?" asked Aarushi. I was so engrossed in the romance that I forgot to ask her about it.

"Yes, please tell me. Was everything okay? Did Himanshu or the warden tried to contact you?" I asked her.

"Everything was okay. I copied all the videos in the pen-drive and went to the police station. It was around four in the evening. You remember the policeman who asked us for the penalty?" asked Aarushi

"Yes. Was that rascal there?" I enquired.

"Yes. His name is Gajendera Mahto. When I told him that I came to log a complaint against my warden and Himanshu, his face turned red. He stood from his chair and asked me the reason. I explained the issues, after which he asked me for the pen drive. I denied to give it, but agreed to copy that in the computer, which was there at the police station. Initially, he denied logging the FIR stating that the videos are morphed, but later when I threatened him that I would complaint to his higher authorities, he agreed to take my statement. Later, while giving me the copy of FIR he warned me not to publicize the issue in public or else I will have to bear the consequences of it. I told him, to start the investigation and need not to worry about me. That rascal thought, I would take the complaint back after getting threatened," explained Aarushi. Though, I knew she was a strong girl, but I was afraid Himanshu would try to harm her.

"Aarushi, just take care of yourself. You need not to go outside until I arrive. I don't want to hear anything. Promise me that you will not go out of your room," I ordered her.

Aarushi remained silent for a while and later she promised me that she would just walk from her room to my flat at evening to execute the surprise she had planned.

"I will ask Nikhil to help me out with the stuffs. I won't go out. Is that okay?" asked Aarushi. I sighed and agreed to her statement.

"Okay. Now I need to leave for the Airport. See you soon," I said. Saurabh and Shakti had already boarded the bus and they were yelling at me to get on the bus.

"Okay. Come soon. I am waiting. Bye," said Aarushi and we hung up the call.

The bus dropped us at the Mysore Railway station. Now it was time for the three of us to depart for our respective destinations. Saurabh had to go to Mumbai and Shakti had to catch a train to Chennai. Initially, I too decided to board a train to Bangalore, but failing to get any confirm ticket, I opted to travel by bus. After Saurabh and Shakti left to catch their train, I took an auto to the bus stand. Luckily, a bus to Bangalore was all set to start its trip. I quickly boarded the bus and relaxed myself on the allocated seat. Fortunately, the bus was sleeper. I didn't realize when I slept.

"*Bhaiya*, Bangalore Airport," said the conductor shaking my arms. I woke up and looked at the watch. I had been sleeping for almost five hours. I was such a crocodile. I thanked the conductor for waking me up and rushed to the airport. I had the flight at 9:00 PM to Delhi. I called Aarushi to know about her whereabouts. She was a bit busy in arrangements and asked me to call her when I arrive at Delhi airport. Nikhil was helping her with all outdoor work. I spent sometime roaming around before the check-in started. The excitement in my heart was increasing with every passing second. I boarded the flight and sat on the allocated window seat. If you have to see the beauty of Delhi, always prefer a window seat while you are flying to Delhi. Delhi looks amazingly beautiful when you look at it from the sky. It is nothing less than a feast to eyes. It took me another two hours to arrive at Delhi Airport.

Shall I buy something for Aarushi as a gift? I asked to myself. *Yes, you should. After all she is going to express her love to you.* My heart answered the question. I looked around at the airport for a jewellery shop. There was a Swarovski showroom at the terminal. It was the first time I was going to buy jewellery. I was worried if Aarushi would like my choice or not.

"Good evening Sir, how may I help you?" asked a lady dressed in a saree. Her nameplate read, Seema.

"Good evening Seema. I want to buy a ring," I said. Seema smiled and said, "There are very few customers who say our name to interact. Generally they just treat us as a helper," she said.

"I completely agree. Would you mind suggesting me a beautiful ring? I don't want it to be much expensive, honestly. I am saying this because, neither of us should be wasting each other's time," I said smiling. Seema asked me to accompany her to the ring counter.

"I am sorry, I forgot to ask. Are you looking a ring for yourself or?" asked Seema and looked at me for an answer. I giggled, and said, "Fiancé".

Seema showed me some budgeted rings and

suggested her favourite ones. To me, all the rings looked beautiful. I was amused to see so much variety. Finally, I asked Seema to choose one and pack. She thought for a while and picked the best one among the options available and packed it in a beautiful case.

"Trust me Sir, your lady is going to love it. And if she doesn't, you can get this ring exchanged at any Swarovski showroom," assured Seema handing me the case. I thanked her for her help and kept the case in my bag. It was 11:45 pm by the time I came out of the Airport. I took a cab to my flat and was highly excited to meet my love. I lowered the window of the cab to get the fresh air in. The cool breeze falling over my face was making me relaxed. It was the best day, I thought. My dream job and my dream girl, both were with me today. Every moment, I spent with Aarushi flashed before my eyes. Though, those were the struggling days, but they were wonderful. The success matters only when you struggle to achieve it.

I called Aarushi to check what she was doing.

"Hey, I will be there knocking the door in another half an hour," I said.

"Really?" asked Aarushi. She sounded worried.

"Yes. Why? Don't you want me to come?" I asked.

"Are you stupid? I am yet to record. I don't have guts to express my feeling on your face. Let's cut the call. I need to start recording. I have asked Nikhil to get some snacks and drinks, so that I get some time alone to record," she said and we hung up the call.

I thought, the time has come when I should inform my parents regarding Aarushi and my relationship. I was a little worried as they would get furious on me for updating them so late. Though, I was confident about their acceptance. They had always been an awesome support. I dialed my mom's number.

"Finally, you remembered that your parents are still alive," taunted my mom.

"*Namaste Ma.* It's nothing like that. I wanted to give you a great news, so I was waiting for this day," I said trying to pacify my mom's anger.

"What is that great news?" she asked.

"I have been selected in the Indian Air Force. Now very soon, you will be a mother of Flight Lieutenant Aaryan Rathod," I said with a pride. My mom could not believe my words for a moment. She asked me again to confirm.

"Are you serious?"

"Yes Ma, I am. I am on my way from Airport to the flat. I was there in Mysore selection board for the last five days," I said to justify my selection. My mom blessed me for my achievement.

"Congratulations *Beta* (Son)! This is a great news," said my dad. He was sitting beside mom all this time and listening to our conversation. I greeted him and thanked him for all the support he had extended to me.

"So is there anything else you would like us to know?" asked Mom. I smelled something fishy. *Does she knows about Aarushi?* I thought.

"Aah… nothing," I said.

"Are you sure? Or, are you planning to update your marital status on Facebook and later tag us," taunted mom. She knew about Aarushi. I was damn sure, it was Nikhil who would have told her about Aarushi. Nikhil was such a rascal.

"No, I wanted to tell you and dad about Aarushi," I said.

"Okay we are listening. Start," my mom ordered.

"I… I mean she… no I mean both of us," I said wondering from how to start.

"Aaryan, relax. You need not act so formal with us. Open up," said Dad. He was the coolest dad on earth. He was the first one who had offered me a peg of scotch when I was leaving my home for higher studies.

Offering me the drink he said, *"I know, you are going to drink once you are out of home. But remember my son, it's okay to drink alcohol in limits, but never let the alcohol drink you."*

"Hmm... actually I love Aarushi. It started a few months back. I was the one who initiated all these. She is an amazing girl, dad. I am sure, both of you are going to like her. She is a very decent, mature and beautiful girl. And she is very studious too. She had given her IAS mains exams and I am sure that she would clear it," I praised about Aarushi.

"Looks like someone is already mad about her!" taunted my mom. I sighed and requested her not to tease me.

"Okay. So, I believe you want this marriage to be arranged under our guidance, right?" asked mom.

"Of course. I can never marry without you guys standing by my side blessing us," I confirmed her.

"Sounds good. At least he has got some cultural values," said Mom.

"You can give us her dad's number. We will initiate the talks," said Dad. The time to shock my parents arrived. I sighed.

"Her dad is no more. She lost her dad during her childhood," I said. There was silence at the other end of the call. Perhaps they were shocked to hear that.

"That is sad. Do you have her mother's number?" asked Dad. I was going to drop another atom bomb on them.

"She lost her mother too. She is an orphan," I said. Three of us, didn't exchange a single word for minutes. Finally my mom started showing her concern in the most diplomatic way.

"Aaryan, I understand that Aarushi had been

through lots of challenges in her life, but you are our only son. And you deserve someone better. How would we ever know her family background? These are required in arrange marriages. I understand that you must have felt sympathy for Aarushi, and that could have been a driving factor for you to fall in love with her. But this is your life Aaryan. Not all decisions of life are made with emotions," said mom. I remained silent and waited for dad to advise me next.

"Look beta, we have never denied your choice. But this time, we are forced to. We have a social status, and no matter what you say, everyone living in a society is ought to maintain his status. Who knows their family has some medical legacy? Might be she also gets prone to it later. How would you manage then? We can't see you struggling whole life," said Dad. I could understand, being parents, it would have been tough for them to accept Aarushi as my match. But, I was no way prepared to give up.

"Ma, Papa. I know it is tough for you to accept this match, but trust me, once you meet her, you would hardly care about the social status. And moreover, can anyone of you guarantee that the girl whom you choose for me would never get a medical issue? Why should I be even bothered about something which no one can guarantee? And I don't care about society. They are not the ones, who made me what I am today. All I want is your support. Aarushi's parents didn't die out of medical issues, but they died in an unfortunate accident. I have to get married to someone, then why not the one whom I love? Even if something wrong happens in future, at least I will be satisfied that it was my decision and I won't be blaming you for it. Please understand, there is no sympathy in this relation. Aarushi is a girl who never took anyone's sympathy. She is brave and confident. I would be lucky to get married to her. Please Papa, Please Ma, just consider it as my last persistence and fulfil it," I begged. My parents must have felt helpless as they agreed for this match on a condition that they would first talk to Aarushi and then finalize our wedding.

"I bet, once you meet her, you would be forcing me to get married to her," I said. While I was still on call, I saw Nikhil's number appearing over my cell phone. He was trying to call me. I was just a kilometre away from my home, so I thought I would rather give them surprise then updating them about my whereabouts.

"Nikhil is calling me. He has planned a party for my success," I didn't include Aarushi's name as that would have raised another hundred questions.

"Great! But don't drink," said Mom. My dad argued to her and said, "Drink in limits. It's your day afterall."

"Sure. Okay Papa, Ma, I need to get down now. I will call you later. Bye," I said and later we hung up the call.

"Bhaiya the road is blocked," said the cab driver who was struggling to find enough space among the parked cars and an approaching Ambulance.

"Bhaiya, I can walk from here. It's just two minutes. But please, give way to the ambulance. Take your cab aside," I requested the driver stepping out of the cab.

"Okay. I will then take reverse and go. Thanks," said the driver and reversed his car. I prayed for the life inside the ambulance and ran towards my flat. I saw some lighting decorations done at the balcony. It really made me feel special. Even lord Rama would not have received that kind of welcome after his glorious victory over Ravana.

Though my flat looked illuminated, but I was surprised to see that none of the street lights were glowing. Even the girls' hostel lights were off.

Why everyone has switched off their lights? Or is it like, all the girls from the hostel are at my flat to witness my love story? I wondered. My heartbeat increased with every step I took towards my flat. I jumped two stairs at a time and rang the doorbell. As no one opened the door, I rang it again. This time without break. Later when I didn't hear anyone sound, I kicked the door. To my shock, it was already opened.

There was blood over the floor. Suddenly my eyes fell on the torn pieces of clothes scattered around the room. I realised it was the same dress Aarushi had wore when we went to the club. The thought of Aarushi wearing the dress made me emotional. 'She would have worn this for me'. I rushed inside the room looking for Aarushi. I yelled her name, but got no response. I was shattered. I sat on the floor which was drenched in blood. I lost the battle to control my tears and cried loudly, but there was no one to hear me. The room was decorated with heart shaped balloons, colorful ribbons and decorative lights. A cake was scattered all over the floor, along with broken pieces of beer bottles. I knew something ill had happened with Aarushi, but was wondering where was she. I gathered strength to stand and walk near the table. Aarushi's cellphone was kept on the table and it was still in recording mode. I stopped the recording and before I could have played it, Nikhil called me again.

"Hello Aaryan," said Nikhil. He sounded panicked and was breathing heavily.

"Where is Aarushi," I asked in a low tone. I was losing my breath.

"Aaryan, she is in ambulance. I and Swati are with her. We are taking her to AIIMS," replied Nikhil. I could not believe that the ambulance which I saw, was carrying Aarushi.

"Is she okay? There is blood all over the floor. Please say she is fine," I cried

"Aaryan, please. You have to be strong. She will be okay. Just come to the hospital," said Nikhil. I hung up the call, took Nikhil's bike key, Aarushi's cell phone and rushed downstairs. My tears dried and there was prayer for Aarushi on my lips. I drove insanely and within fifteen minutes I was there at AIIMS. I parked the bike and called Nikhil. He informed me that Aarushi was admitted in ICU and not more than one visitor was allowed.

"Swati and I will come downstairs. You can go and visit Aarushi," said Nikhil. I rushed towards the ICU.

"Wait, you can't enter inside," said a nurse stopping me from entering the ICU where Aarushi was admitted.

"Please Sister, let me go. She needs me," I begged.

"All she needs is a team of doctor and prayers. Moreover, she is not in a state to talk or even open her eyes to look at you. So you better wait outside. Doctors are coming, give them a way," said the nurse pushing me out of the operation theatre, when she saw the team of doctors approaching the operation theatre. I was so helpless that I fell under the feet of one of the doctors pleading him to save Aarushi.

"Please, don't do this. We are here to save her, rest all depends on God's will. Please get aside and allow us to carry on our job," said the doctor raising me up. I tried to peek inside the operation room, when the nurse opened the door for the doctors.

Aarushi was lying unconsciously over the bed with an oxygen mask covering her mouth. Her head was covered with bandage. Scars on her face were visible even from the distance. She must have gone through lots of pains. I stood there watching her, until I was pushed out of the room. All our memories flashed before me. The girl, whom I loved more than anything else, was lying over the bed fighting for life. Devastated, I sat over the bench placed outside the operation theatre. Doctors started operating as the bulb outside the theatre was on. I was feeling restless and wanted to cry my heart out. I went to the washroom and locked myself inside. That was the day, I last cried. I was blaming myself for everything. Had I not spent time at the airport for buying the ring, Aarushi would not have been in the hospital. Lost in Aarushi's memories and prayers for her quick recovery, I realised Aarushi's phone must have recorded everything that had happened with her in my room.

I took out the cellphone and went to the hospital terrace, hiding myself from getting caught. I played the recording.

"Hmm… yaar kya bolu (what shall i say). Okay, let me start now. Aahh.. It is quite tough for me. Don't know how people say it so easily. Anyway, enough of nonsense. Now let's come to the point.

Listen, I may not be as good as you in gelling up the words to make them sound beautiful, but all these words which I am going to say are directly from my heart. The first day when you saw me at the terrace, I really wanted to spit on your face and slap you for your misdeed. All your shayaris irritated me to the core of my heart. For me it was just my dream to clear IAS and live a normal life. I had never thought, I would fall in love with someone. This love was never planned, but it happened, and now you are the most beautiful gift I have in my life.

The way you look at me, care for me, makes me feel special. I started dreaming a wonderful life with you. Now, I listen to love songs, and I even sing whenever I am alone at room. I imagine you while I sing those songs.

I don't know what makes me so special for you that you love me like an insane. I can't explain how I feel every time when you are near me. Many a times I felt like hugging you in my arms and locking your lips with mine, but I stopped myself every time. But today, I am not going to stop myself from pouring my love on you. I don't care what destiny has planned for me; I have decided to follow my heart. I have seen worst times in my life, and nothing else can supersede it. Now I have been awarded a new life, and I want to live it with you.

I don't know what else to say. I just want you to believe my words. I love you. I love you Aaryan. I will never leave you and promise me that you too would be with me always and forever.

Before you come running to kiss me, or if I say in your words, to eat me, make sure, neither Nikhil nor Swati are there in the room, else, I won't be comfortable. I am dying to kiss you, love you and hug you. Please come soon, your Aarushi is waiting.

Knock, knock…

"Aaryan? Nikhil? Swati?" (asked Aarushi)

"Come on say, who's there?" Knock, knock…

I know it's you Aaryan… wait I am opening the door. The door opens.

"Aaaaaaaahhhhhhh…" (Himanshu kicked on Aarushi's belly as soon as she opened the door)

Close the door…hold her hands.

"Himanshu leave me alone. You are such a coward. Aaryan is on his way. He will kill you. Dare not touch me. Pull off your hands from me."

"How dare you log a complaint against me? You have got all the videos, now I will show you the live telecast," Himanshu warned her.

"Noooooo…."yelled Aarushi while Himanshu tore her dress.

"Aaaah.. bitch…She bite my hands," yelled Himanshu.

"Leave me Himanshu. Don't do this," cried Aarushi. Himanshu stared at Aarushi and grinned, scaring the hell out of her.

"Switch off the lights," ordered Himanshu to one of his companions. Aarushi's breath was caught in her throat.

"Who the hell you think you are? Aaryan will soon be here... He is not going to leave you. Go away...huh.. huh... go..," stammered Aarushi. Then someone broke a bottle, and said, "Bhaiya, insert this in her stomach."

"No... don't do this. Don't... aaaaaahhhhhh," yelled Aarushi. I could hear the slap sound. Later I heard, sounds of bottles falling on the floor, people running around. Perhaps Aarushi had skipped the grip of the goon, who held her arms.

"*Maar saali ko, rod se maar* (hit this bitch with the rod)," yelled Himanshu. The next second, heart skipped a beat when I heard Aarushi's scream while she felt on the floor after being hit by the rod.

"Bhaiya, she is still alive," said one among those bastards.

"Lit the lighter," ordered Himanshu.

"Please leave me.. huuuh... huuh.. don't do this... kill me if you want... but don't ... huuuh...," mumbled Aarushi.

Someone slapped her brutally and said, "Can't you shut your mouth? Himanshu Bhaiya is making his mood. Don't dare to disturb him while he is drinking."

Aarushi was stunned. She was slapped again and again. Though I could hear Aarushi's struggle to fight back, but having been hit by the rod and on stomach, she hardly had enough strength to protect herself.

"Where are you Aaryan? Please come,... please Aaryan," cried Aarushi.

Tears from my eyes refused to stop while I kept listening to the recording. I felt like jumping from the hospital's terrace and suicide for not being there when

Aarushi needed me the most.

"Both of you make her ready for sex. Take each and every cloth off from her body. Let me show her my masculinity," said Himanshu. Aarushi was scared and she yelled for help. A shiver went through my body when I heard the scream of Aarushi, while the two monsters were tearing off each cloth from her body. She fought to save herself. She yelled for help, but everything went in vain. She cried, but later her mouth was stuffed and hands were tied with the torn pieces of her dress. Now she could not even yell anymore for help. Aarushi's heart pounded in her chest, but her weak body could not support her. She knew that something terrible was going to happen to her.

"Rajan, after *Bhaiya Ji*, I will go next on her. She has troubled me a lot," said one of the guy holding Aarushi. His companions called Himanshu as *Bhaiya Ji*.

"Okay… okay. Both of you will get your chance," said Himanshu. I could hear Aarushi's struggle to scream. Himanshu pushed himself inside Aarushi. Her lifeless body pounded for a fraction of a second. She could not even scream to voice her horrendous pain. Her screams died in her throat. I could hear them laugh and doing cheers while Himanshu kept giving thrust inside Aarushi.

"I am done. Aaaahhhh… It was quite a hard work. But I loved the heat she carries with her. Rajan, it's your time to have some fun with her," said Himanshu.

There was no one to listen to Aarushi's scream when she yelled for help. And now when she couldn't scream anymore as her mouth was stuffed to close, I know she must have been looking at her God to help her out. But that night even God refused to save her child. God behaved like humans, meek and quiet towards injustice.

"Bhaiya ji, Joginder is calling," said Rajan. Joginder must have been a friend of Himanshu.

"Okay. We will leave now. Rajan is having fun with her now," said Himanshu and laughed.

"Hey Balli, we have got very less time, go and get your piece of flesh. We have to leave now as Nikhil is on his way to the flat. He may come here anytime. Pass me the broken bottle," ordered Himanshu. Balli was the third guy accompanying Himanshu. It was all blur for Aarushi. I could not even imagine how she would have survived that insufferable pain. Aarushi's pain didn't matter much for the barbarians blinded by lust and overpowered by alcohol. They continued to tear her apart.

"Balli, now stop and pass me the broken bottle," ordered Himanshu. Aarushi's bleeding body was lying there motionless.

"Bhaiya Ji, shall we not ask her last wish? Let me take clothes out of her mouth,"

"Aahhh..huuuh… huuuh… huuuh.. .uuhhh..," struggled Aarushi to take a breath.

"Let me tell you before I kill you. Even if your Aaryan files a rape and murder allegation against me, nothing wrong can happen to me. My dad has power and money, which are the two most important factors to play around with rules of laws. And moreover, I am still under eighteen. So, even if the charges are proved against me, which won't happen though, I would hardly get three years sentence and that too, being a politician son, I would be treated nicely inside the jail. This is India my darling, laws and rules are for poor, not for people like us. Do you have a last wish?" asked Himanshu.

"Thuuuuuuuu…" Aarushi spitted on Himanshu's face.

"I do have… a … last wish. But, you are a coward and …hhhuuhh... a ..coward can't fulfil anyone's wish. I will ask Aaryan to… fulfil my last wish. Aaryan… I love you.. I may not be able to survive, but promise me that you won't....*huuhh*...*huuuh*.. leave Himanshu alive. Kill him the day you know what he did to me. I love you Aaryan. Wish you would have been here. I am sorry. Your Aarushi left you in between. Forgive me..," screamed Aarushi out of pain.

"Bitch, I will show what I can do," yelled Himanshu, "How does this broken bottle feels inside your vagina," he bullied her.

I was stunned to hear that. My body froze. Thereafter, all I could hear was Aarushi's scream when her body was pierced with glasses, tortured by slaps and hit by rods.

A lovely, innocent soul had been torn apart under the sky which is said to be ruled by, God. The girl, who always stood for right things, had seen only wrong things happening to her.

Aarushi's last wish to kill Himanshu was echoing in my ears. I gathered strength to stand and walk to the operation theatre. Nikhil and Swati were standing before the operation theatre waiting for doctors to come out. Nikhil ran to me when he saw my devastated state. I hugged him and cried my heart out.

"Aaryan, please don't do this. You need to be strong. Aarushi has no one except you," sympathized Nikhil. Swati too assured me that everything would be fine.

"There is someone who can help me," I said taking my cell phone out. I wanted to talk to the lady astrologer who had been guiding me all these times. I dialled her number.

"Why are you calling me?" said Swati when she saw my number appearing on her cell phone. I was stunned to realize that the lady whom I believed to be an astrologer was none other than Swati.

"I was calling the lady astrologer," I said looking into Swati's eyes. She stood froze and didn't know how to react. Nikhil, who was unaware of the lady astrologer, asked me what was I trying to do. Swati stood silent. I could see tears dropping from her eyes.

"Excuse me," said the doctor. The operation was over and the team of doctors operating Aarushi came out of the operation theatre. Nikhil, Swati and I ran towards them to know Aarushi's condition.

"How is she doctor?" I asked trying to peek inside the operation room.

"Relax. We can't say anything right now. She has been tortured brutally. Most of her internal organs are damaged. There were broken glass pieces in her vagina. She has been raped brutally. Her skull is also fractured. It seems a rod or something hit her. As of now, we need to monitor her condition for another two days before we can operate her again. I sympathize with you and trust me; we are doing the best we can. Rest all depends on God's wish. Never in my life I have seen such a strong girl. She is a fighter," said the doctor. I knew what Aarushi had been through. I knew who was responsible for this. And somewhere, I knew what I had to do next.

"Doctor, we have informed the police and the media channels. They will be here anytime," said the nurse accompanying the team of doctors. We were asked to wait in the lobby until the media and police arrives.

I pleaded the doctor to allow me to see Aarushi once. After seeing my devastated condition, he felt mercy on me and allowed me to see her from a distance and gave me a time limit of two minutes. I knew, these were my last two minutes with Aarushi. I wiped my tears, opened the door and entered inside.

Aarushi was covered with a white cloth till her neck. Her head was bandaged and there were several monitors and drips connected to her body. It was tough for me to believe my eyes. It was tough to see her laying over the bed fighting for her life. My feet wanted to run and hug her till my last breath, but I stopped myself at a distance.

"Aarushi, I am sorry. I am sorry; I was not there with you when you needed me the most. I will never ever forgive myself for this. You have to fight this battle for us. You can't give up. You have never given up. I need you Aarushi. I love you. You can't leave me alone. I won't be able to survive without you. I will not leave those bastards alive. Trust me, I don't care what would happen to me once I murder them, all that matters to me now is, justice for you. I have been given two minutes to live my entire life with you. These doctors don't know that this is perhaps our last meet. There are thousands of shayari waiting to be recited for you. I am going to vomit all those shayaris once we get married. Please, don't give up on our dreams," I could not hold my tears anymore and cried loud. Nurse rushed inside the room and dragged me out.

"Are you insane? Don't you know this is ICU? You have to maintain silence. Now all three of you need to go down at the lobby and wait," whispered Nurse. Nikhil and Swati held me and forcefully dragged me to the lobby.

"I am fine. Leave me," I said asking them to set me free from their grip.

"Aaryan, we need to tell the police about Himanshu. I am sure, he is the one who has done this with Aarushi," suggested Swati. Nikhil seconded her.

I knew, the police on whom Swati and Nikhil were showing trust, was nothing more than a puppet of Himanshu's powerful father. Himanshu was correct, law and order is just for common people and not for powerful idiots. And moreover, knowing the juvenile act of our constitution, I knew, even if Himanshu is held guilty for rape, he would be set free to live freely in society again. Vote hungry politicians will debate on media channels defending Himanshu's innocence and ultimately, it will be Aarushi who would be at the losing end. Why in our country, it is always the victim who ends up being the loser? It is quite tough to digest, but it is true that our society accepts a rapist but not a rape victim.

"Aaryan, police has arrived," said Nikhil when he saw the police van near the hospital entrance. Swati rushed to a police officer to detail out the situation. The police officer looked hardly bothered about the incident and asked Swati to relax. He was expecting us to relax and explain him the horrendous story. I was sure he was not there to find the clue to catch the culprit as he already knew who the culprit was. I was in a dilemma if I should log an FIR against Himanshu or should I just go ahead, punish him to death.

I knew, killing Himanshu would destroy my professional career, personal life, my parents' image and everything else I had built up till date. But, not punishing him for his misdeed would be like living a life as a dead soul. I stood motionless, lost in my thoughts. The selfish side of me was asking me to forget Aarushi and leave everything to the law. But what about the promises I made to Aarushi? What about the trust she showed on me? What about her last wish? I was now very much assured what I needed to do.

I escaped from the lobby without informing Nikhil. I knew, if I would have told him my plans, he would have never let me go out of the hospital. I hired an auto outside AIIMS and left.

"Where you need to go?" asked the auto-driver switching the meter on.

"Just keep driving. I will tell you later. I will pay you hundred bucks more than the actual meter reading," I replied as I was not sure where I could find Himanshu. The auto-driver looked puzzled, but as I promised to pay him extra bucks, he started the journey. I was wondering, who could help me get Himanshu's whereabouts and then I realized Salim would be the best person to ask. Salim had good contacts in the city, so it was a bit easy task for him to find Himanshu's location.

"Hello Salim," I called Salim to enquire about Himanshu.

"Aaryan Bhaiya," said Salim. He sounded depressed.

"I am going to ask you for two things. You are free to deny any help and cut the call," I said in a firm tone. I never wanted to pressurise him to support me.

"*Bhaiya*, you can ask me for anything. I am ready to do anything for you. I heard about Aarushi. Trust me Bhaiya, had I been there at that moment I would have killed those bastards. But, due to my mother's ill health, I left for Aligarh this morning," he reasoned. "I understand, I want to know where can I find Himanshu at this time? Also, I need a butcher knife. I know you have a friend who works at a butcher shop," I told him.

Salim could not utter a single word for minutes. We both remained silent until I said, "Fine. I will find him. Thanks for all your help."

"*Bhaiya* wait," said Salim stopping me from dropping the call.

"*Bhaiya*, I know what you are going through, but are you sure you want to do this? You have your own life, why do you want to destroy it?" continued Salim.

"My life is struggling for life at the hospital bed," I replied. Salim took a pause, and said, "Okay. Give me ten minutes, I will call you back with all information." I thanked him for his help and later we dropped the call.

Meanwhile, I received a call from Nikhil. At first I decided to drop it, but later I thought, maybe it was our last interaction. I was on a mission where there were chances that I might not return alive.

"Hello," I said picking up the call.

"Where the hell are you?" yelled Nihil

"What happened?" I asked avoiding his question.

"Aaryan, tell me where are you?" he asked again.

"I am going to meet Himanshu. I need to do justice with Aarushi," I replied. Nikhil was stunned to hear that.

"Are you a judge? Who are you to do justice? Do you know the consequences of it? You have been selected in the Indian Air Force. Don't forget it was your dream. You will spoil everything Aaryan. Don't be stupid," he blasted.

"I know the consequences. I know that I am no one to do justice. But I am forced to do it. If I won't, then that rascal would be living free in society and Aarushi would never get justice. What shall I do? Wait for our law to change the juvenile act, which currently looks at age and not the level of crime? Whom should I trust? The police force, which is nothing more than a puppet at the hands of Himanshu's dad.

You are right, the Indian Air force was my dream, but to see me in the uniform was Aarushi's dream too. She was the one who used to pray daily for my success. We have lived hundreds of dreams together. I don't want to live any of those dreams alone. And it's not just for Aarushi, it's also for those girls who have been victim of Himanshu in the past, and trust me if this bastard happens to live for a few more years, then there will be hundreds of other girls facing the same fate as Aarushi's. And moreover, now I don't care about the consequences. I have nothing more to lose, so I am the most powerful now," I explained.

"Aaryan, think about Aarushi. She is lying on the bed fighting for life. You are leaving her alone when she needs you the most," said Nikhil.

"She is a strong girl. I know she won't give up. And

she knows that I am with her always. I need to drop the call now, bye," I said and cut the call before Nikhil would have tried again to convince me to stop.

Salim had tried to call on my cell phone, but as I was busy on call with Nikhil, he dropped me a message.

"Himanshu is at Tasmac Bar. Connaught place. There is one more guy accompanying him, my friend, Suresh, who works at that bar, will get you the knife. But Bhaiya, I still beg you, don't do this." I simply wrote thanks to him.

"Bhaiya, drop me at the Tasmac bar at Connaught place," I said to the auto-driver. He had heard my conversations with Salim and Nikhil, so he was bit hesitant to face me or ask any question. He might have considered me as a psycho killer. Silently, he dropped me at the bar, took the fare and left.

I was standing at the entrance of the bar. Hundreds of things were making round in my thoughts. Never in my dreams had I thought, I would be killing someone someday. My feet were frozen, I was paralysed. Later, I took a deep breath and as most of the engineers say, "*Jo hoga dekha jayega* (Let it be whatever it be)" I entered the bar.

"Are bhaiya, bahar aaiye (Brother, please come out)," said someone pulling me by my arms. I was shocked to see an unknown person behaving in such a manner. I was about to punch hard on his face when he said, "*Aap Aaryan bhiaya hai na* (Aren't you Aaryan?)"

"How do you know me," I asked.

"I am Suresh. Salim told me about you" he said.

"How did you recognise me?" I asked suspiciously as I had never met him before.

"This bar is mostly visited by its regular customers. I have been working here for the past eight years and I know everyone," replied Suresh wiping his sweat with his sleeves.

"Great. So you must be knowing why I am here?" I

asked.

"Yes, I got to know it from Salim. Whatever happened to Aarushi bhabhi is really unforgivable. But, I know, you are not a kind of a man who should kill someone, so please think again if you really want to do this," he showed concern.

"Where can I get a knife?" I didn't want to explain anything to anyone. I knew what was going through in my heart at that moment. Suresh realized that there was no point convincing me anymore.

"I am going to the kitchen, which is at the backside. I will drop the knife from the window. Himanshu is sitting on the left side corner table. He is accompanied by one more person. As you have already decided, so let me tell you. Don't waste time talking to him. Just kill him and leave," said Suresh and left for the kitchen. I sighed and as guided by Suresh, went to the backside of the bar. Soon, Suresh dropped the butcher knife from the window. I picked the knife and hide it inside my shirt.

It was time for me to enter the bar. I could feel the sounds of my heartbeat. My whole body was sweating. I knew, if I would have waited for another minute to pass, I could have stepped back. I took a deep breath and walked towards the corner table, trying to push away the thoughts of what might be the consequences.

The bar had decent amount of customers that day. Had Suresh not informed me about Himanshu's table, it could have been a trouble for me to spot my prey. I saw Himanshu from a distance.

I noticed that, Himanshu was showing some clips to his friends on his mobile. They both were laughing loud and enjoying the show. I slowly went near his table. They were so engrossed in watching the video that they could not even notice my presence. Before I could have taken out the knife and slit his throat, I happened to peek into the clip which was being played on Himanshu's mobile. That bastard was showing the recorded tape he had made while he and his two other friends' brutually raped Aarushi. I stood frozen with rallies of tears in my eyes. I could see them slapping Aarushi and stuffing her mouth with torn pieces of her clothes.

"*Ma*******, (motherfucker)," I yelled and took the knife outside my shirt. Himanshu turned back and before he could have reacted, I passed the knife across his throat. Blood started oozing out of his throat. It was all over the table, my shirt, my face, but I didn't stop. My body was possessed by anger and revenge. I wanted to make him feel the pain Aarushi had to go through because of him.

Himanshu's friend managed to escape from the bar. Within a few seconds, the entire bar was emptied. There were just two persons inside, the dead and the murderer. Yes, I knew, this is how people would remember me.

I was lying in a pool of blood in the corner of the bar with Himanshu, who was already punished to death. Somewhere, I had become a psycho as I was not having the satisfaction of seeing Himanshu dying so soon. I wanted him to stay alive for a few more minutes so that I could cut him into pieces and make him realize what it felt to Aarushi when he and two of his friends were inserting bottles in her organs. Aarushi's painful voice, her helpless cry was echoing in my ears. I went mad and beheaded Himanshu. I had killed the body, now I was killing the soul. Lost in Aarushi's thought, I kept chopping Himanshu. I was not what I was anymore. My whole body was drained in blood. Rallies of tears were flowing from my eyes. With every cut on Himanshu's body that I made, my heart was feeling lighter. I was having a sense of relief that no matter what happens now, Aarushi got justice.

News of the horrific killing of MLA's son spread

like fire. Gajendera too got informed about the incident. He contacted the local patrol police to arrest me and collect evidence from the crime scene. Drenched in blood, I looked at the policeman who came to arrest me inside the bar. He looked frightened.

I looked at the policeman and told him pointing at Himanshu's mutilated body, "Ask his dad to bring a bag along with him. He has to collect the pieces not the body of his rapist son."

Later, I spit on Himanshu's body and raised my hands in air to allow the policeman to perform his duty. The policeman slowly stepped forward and handcuffed me. He also took the knife and Himanshu's mobile and placed them in plastic pouches. A lot of people stood outside the bar were recording everything. No one really cared to know the truth.

Meanwhile, Gajendera too arrived at the scene. He furiously approached me and hit me hard on my face. Though it did hurt me, but I laughed to make him realize, how weak he was.

"I can understand your anger. After all, the person who used to feed you bones is no more. You son of a bitch," I said looking into Gajendera's eyes. Had there been no audiences capturing everything in their cell phones, Gajendera would have shot me on the spot.

I was dragged and pushed inside the rear seat of the patrolling jeep and taken to the police station, which came under Gajendera's rule. Without interrogating anything, three of the police staffs, including Gajendera, started hitting me with belts and rods. I got several injuries and fractures. It was almost impossible for me to stand as the rod broke my ankle of both the feet. Unable to stand anymore, I fell down on the floor. Various parts of my body were bleeding. Realizing that I may die in the police station itself, they stopped hitting me anymore. After a few minutes, Gajendera came up with a register book and asked me to sign under some statement. I didn't have enough strength to open my eyes and read what was written on that paper.

"You don't have any other option than to sign it. If you want your girl's safety then better sign it because you don't know the influence of Dayal Joshi. And moreover, you have killed his son. You will die anyway. All you can do now is let that girl live a few more days," said Gajendera holding me by my hair.

I somehow gathered enough strength to read the statements.

"During initial investigation, Aaryan Rathod agreed that he raped Aarushi and attempted to murder her. Aaryan first won the trust of Aarushi and promised to marry her, but on the night of August 7, while Aarushi was at Aaryan's home preparing for a party, Aaryan came drunk and abused Aarushi. Aarushi, who was shocked to see Aaryan's behavior tried to escape out of the room, but Aaryan hit Aarushi's head with the beer bottle, which he had in his hand. Later, he took the broken glass piece of the beer bottle and slit Aarushi's throat. Aaryan was so overpowered with alcohol that, even after Aarushi was bleeding over the floor, he raped Aarushi brutally. He also inserted beer bottles inside her private parts. Realizing he may get caught, he tried to flee away from the spot. Himanshu Joshi was informed about the incident from locals. Himanshu tracked the location of Aaryan and came to know that the latter was sitting in the Tasmac bar at Connaught place. When Himanshu reached there and asked Aaryan to surrender to the police, Aaryan took the knife which he was carrying along with himself, and brutally killed Himanshu Joshi."

"Are you done reading? And even if you are not, I don't have much time for this. Hold this pen and sign it," ordered Gajendera forcing a pen inside my fist. I knew, I had no option and Dayal Joshi, being an MLA, could have done anything to Aarushi. I had no other option then to sign and take all blames on me. I knew, everyone would hate me for this. No girl would ever trust a man's love. There would be no more faith in love. But, all I did was because I loved Aarushi.

Soon, media was informed that the rapist has been caught. Numbers of TV channels and newspaper reporters gathered in front of the police station to capture my image and ask questions. The police force at the station was struggling to manage the crowd. Without listening to a single word from me, they started airing the story, which was shared to them by Gajendera. Within no time, my image from a software engineer was changed to a rapist and a murderer.

Later, I was carried to the central jail for further proceedings. I was not allowed to meet anyone. There was so much hatred for me that sometimes, I was hit by other prisoners during lunchtime and at night. I wanted to explain the reality to them, but I could not for two reasons. Firstly, no one would have trusted me as I was convicted for rape and murder, and secondly, had Dayal or Gajendera came to know about this, they could have harmed Aarushi. I preferred to remain silent and left everything on destiny.

Though, cases in our country take long to close, but in my case it was a bit different. There was protest in various parts of the country. Everyone was demanding justice for Aarushi. Everyone wanted me to be hanged. People will celebrate my death tomorrow and I really don't care about that. All I want now is that you all realize where we are heading towards as a nation. I want you all to realize that Aaryan was not born to be a murderer, but a good and responsible citizen of India. Just like you, he too had dreams, he too fell in love, but unlike you, he could not get any of those.

I was happy that Aarushi was not alone. Aarushi's well wishers were in millions. I am also, one among them. I want her to live all her dreams which she wished. I want her to love me even when I am not there with her anymore.

I am left with a very few time. So, now I end up writing anymore. But, before I finish, I want to ask a few questions to you.

What I did might not be correct, but before one decides on that, one needs to tell me, what else I could have done? What forced me to do so? And moreover, did I do anything wrong? Did I kill a bright future of the country or a great soul or did I kill a barbarian who had no rights to live? I could have waited for all of you to light candles and do a silent protest at India gate, but tell me what it could have fetched me in return? Tell me how long would you have waited for justice? What justice it would provide to Aarushi? Or I should have waited for law to handle this case and later free Himanshu, because the book of law doesn't allow a juvenile to be arrested for more than three years?

Please, understand this. I will be no more tomorrow, but you will be there around. What if something like this happens to your closed one. Would you still wait for Facebook likes or comments. Trust me you wouldn't, and you would also look for justice. And you can get justice only when the laws are in place. It's time for you to wake up. It's time for us to wake up the government. Aaryan will die tomorrow, but the nation has to wake up.

... signing off
Aaryan

Chapter 17

At the same time in AIIMS

* * *

On the night of December 23, 2013, Delhi didn't sleep. Doctors in AIIMS were giving their best efforts to save Aarushi. Best of the doctors were called to handle Aarushi's case. Entire country was praying for her life, and my death.

"How could a man whom she loved so much raped her so brutally?" was the question asked by each Indian. For them, December 24, 2013, was going to be a historical day of justice.

Media channels, who were covering the story of Aarushi, flashed news saying, "Aarushi is out of comma". This news spread like fire. Within no time, college students, school goers, working professionals, housewives and every human soul came out on the street. Winter was at its peak, but people were on roads distributing colours and crackers among all the volunteers who were fighting for justice for Aarushi. They all looked happy and congratulated each other. It didn't matter if they knew the person standing next to them or walking with them. They had all gathered for a cause that was common to each one of them—justice! That was one word anyone could read on those several hundred banners and posters that the crowd unanimously waived. The young India could have chosen to sleep at their homes inside the warm blanket on chilled winter night, but they instead chose to spend the night on the roads of Delhi till they get to hear news of my death. Every single policeman in the city was on alert. Dressed in khaki, they were trying their best to control the crowd. It was a different Delhi that day—never heard of and certainly never seen earlier. Young India was boiling. Scores of mediapersons and camera persons captured it all and broadcasted it live to the rest of the nation, which participated in the same emotion and aggression through this coverage. Many journalists along with thousands of Aarushi's well-wishers gathered in front of AIIMS to get some more information about Aarushi's health.

The silence in the ICU of AIIMS that evening was loud enough to wake up the entire nation. It was on every news channel. The camera persons covered every movement of the bureaucratic and political cavalcades that arrived at the gate. The world outside AIIMS continued to wait in anticipation.

"Doctor, she wants to say something," shouted a nurse who was inside the ICU monitoring Aarushi's heart beat rate. Senior surgeon Dhanraj Pillai, rushed towards Aarushi and asked her to speak slowly. Aarushi could hardly open her eyes. It was the longest she had slept. The lights inside the ICU were made dim to make Aarushi feel better.

"Aaryan," blabbered Aarushi.

"Don't worry. He is going to be hanged tomorrow. And you will be happy to know that, every Indian is praying for your quick recovery," said the doctor holding hands of Aarushi to make her feel comfortable. Aarushi's eyes popped out when she heard that I was going to be hanged tomorrow. Her heart rate increased and she wanted to shout. The nurse and the doctor both got panicked and could not understand what was happening.

"Aaryan didn't do this to me. Himanshu did," said Aarushi breathing heavily. Dr. Dhanraj was shocked to hear that. The nurse, who was trying to normalise Aarushi, was equally shocked to hear that.

"Why did Aaryan killed Himanshu?" asked the doctor with frown eyes. Aarushi managed to smile and said, "Did he?"

"Yes. Himanshu was killed on the same night when you were admitted here," replied the nurse. Aarushi closed her eyes and a rally of tears came out. She was satisfied to know that I had kept the promise she wanted me to fulfil. She sighed.

"Please save Aaryan. He must live. Himanshu and his two friends raped me. Those bas**** even tried to kill me, but looks like that I got out of comma today only for Aaryan. Please for god sake, save him," cried Aarushi holding hands of the doctor and begging to them for my life. Doctor asked Aarushi to relax and promised to try his best to save me. Nikhil, who always managed to visit Aarushi was peeking inside the glass window in anticipation. He was happy to see Aarushi's recovery.

Dr. Dhanraj came out of the ICU instructing the nurse to look after Aarushi.

"Aarushi said that Aaryan is not the one who damaged her, but Himanshu," said the doctor to Nikhil. Nikhil got tears in his eyes. He nodded his head and said, "I have been saying this for a while, but no one believed me. Aaryan, didn't speak a word in the court fearing Himanshu's dad, Dayal Joshi, would get Aarushi killed inside the hospital itself. And to some extent you too would agree to this point as it is not too tough for a politician," said Nikhil.

"I had heard about love stories, but this is the first time, I am witnessing one. The guy didn't utter a word in his defense and is happily going to get hanged tomorrow, and the girl who was in coma till yesterday, came out of it just to let the whole world know about the truth," said the doctor.

"Doctor, the police have arrived. They need to register the statement of Aarushi," said the nurse who was informed by the receptionist about the arrival of the police.

"Doctor, there is one thing that I must tell you now. We have to protect Aarushi in any case from Dayal and his men. Even police is at their side. Especially, Inspector Gajendera Mahto. He was the one who manipulated the entire story and presented in the court. If he is the one who is coming to take Aarushi's statement, then either we should not allow him to talk to Aarushi or we too should record Aarushi's statement," warned Nikhil. The doctor understood the background of the entire story and hence assured Nikhil that nothing wrong could happen now.

Two of the police personals and a lady police arrived at the ICU. Luckily Gajendera was not among them. Nikhil was asked to stay outside the ICU, while the doctor and officers in *khakhi* entered the ICU to register Aarushi's statement.

"Aarushi, are you okay to talk?" asked the lady inspector. Aarushi struggled to open her eyes. Later, she nodded her head to permit the police to note her statements. God knows, from where she was getting the power to talk in such a pain. She was indeed a very different girl.

Aarushi narrated the whole incident of that unfortunate night. She also shared the incidences that happened in the past with other hostel mates. Warden, Gajendera and everyone else names were noted in the statement. At the end when the police was about to leave, she said one last thing, "Aaryan is not a kind of a man who would kill anyone. He was forced to do it because your police force failed to protect our society from a bastard. Please don't punish him for being a common man. If he dies, the trust on justice will die forever."

The police officer assured Aarushi that he would try his best to get things sorted as soon as possible. He too knew, neither Aarushi, nor I had enough time left. Soon, the officer along with his team left from AIIMS. On their way out, they were insanely chased by news hungry mediapersons, who were standing at the gate of AIIMS hoping to get breaking news for their channels. But, none of the policemen stopped to answer any of the questions thrown on them.

Meanwhile, Aarushi wanted to talk to Nikhil and requested the doctor to allow Nikhil inside the ICU. Doctor thought for a while and later nodded his head to permit on a condition that the meeting should not be for more than five minutes. As soon as Nikhil got the permission, he rushed inside the ICU to see Aarushi.

"I am so glad that you are back in your senses. Aaryan always said that, Aarushi is not a girl who would give up easily. She is a fighter. God, you guys are insane lovers," said Nikhil wiping his tears of happiness. Aarushi struggled to take a breath and said, "How is Aaryan? Do you meet him often? I want to see him," said Aarushi and broke into tears.

"Aarushi please, control yourself. It is a miracle that you came out of comma just a few hours before Aaryan's execution. I am sure, you guys will get justice. Aaryan always asks about you. He never prayed for his success or even for his life, but he prays daily for your quick recovery. You will be surprised to know that he is writing a book to share yours and his love story with the entire nation. He even handed me a note and asked me to pass it you. I make sure I carry it with me daily. It should be somewhere in my pockets. Let me check," said Nikhil hunting for the note in all his pockets. Aarushi had got a cute little smile on her face and she was waiting patiently to read my notes for her.

"Here you go. Shall I read it?" said Nikhil unfolding the piece of paper. Aarushi blinked her eyes to say yes.

"The day when you will know the truth, I may not be there with you, but my soul will always be around you; they will just hand over my body to you," read Nikhil. Aarushi's eyes were filled with tears. She wiped her face with a napkin kept beside her and smiled.

"Nikhil can you pass a note to Aaryan in your next visit to him?" asked Aarushi. Nikhil smiled and took the pen out of his pocket to write.

"I know the truth and I know you will be there with me forever. And dare not even think that you will die. If God needs a life, then it will be mine not yours and let me assure you, my soul will be around you forever. And the day you think of any other girls, I am going to give you and that bitch a nightmare!"

"Aaryan," said Ali Sir, unlocking my cell. I was busy arranging the pages in serial order. I looked at Ali sir, and wondered if he was there to inform me about the process before the execution.

"Ali Sir. What happened? I believe, I still have couple of hours left," I said looking out at the dark sky covered with clouds. It was thundering outside. Perhaps God too felt helpless in front of our judicial system and thought of showing his protest by blanketing the entire sky with black clouds.

"Aarushi is out of comma and she has also registered her statement with the police," said Ali sir. I could not believe my ears. I stood paralysed trying to grasp what Ali sir said. Soon the happiness of my heart flowed as tears from my eyes. I fell on the ground crying loud and thanking god for saving

Aarushi. Ali sir took hold of me and asked me to get ready for appearing in the court.

"Now at this time? Why do you need to take me to the court? Is it a process before executing someone or is there something else the judge wants to know?" I asked wiping my tears.

"As I said, Aarushi has given her statement about Himanshu Joshi and all his partners, who were involved in this crime. The police was able to trace the videos of other sexual harassments that bastard did with innocent girls. Currently a search team has been appointed to catch the hostel warden. It seems she has left the city fearing to get caught. The police inspector, Gajendera has been suspended from the job and an enquiry has been set against him. There was a meeting called by the judge which included other judges from the panel and senior officers of Delhi police who recorded Aarushi's statement. I am not sure about the judgment, but if now I am asked to carry your execution, I will rather resign than follow the rules of law," said Ali sir in a firm tone, looking into my eyes. He didn't promise me, but to himself. I smiled and thanked him for showing his trust on me. I covered myself with the blanket and followed Ali sir to the court.

Unlike most of the times, there was a deep silence inside the court. A couple of police officers occupied the front row and three other judges were sitting at the chairs kept over a podium. I greeted all of them as I entered.

"Aaryan, based on the recent statement registered by the victim girl to the police and all the other evidences, the court decides to revoke your death penalty. The rape charges which were logged against you stand false. But, the murder charges still stand true. The court condemns the act of negligence shown by the Delhi police in the entire event and warns the police to take their duty religiously towards maintaining the law and order. Court also realises the mental

trauma one would have gone through because of the failure of law and order in the city, but that doesn't mean one should take law in one's hand and commit crime. Late Himanshu Joshi is held guilty for rape of the 28-year-old girl. Also, Aaryan Rathod is held guilty to take law in his hands and murder of Himanshu Joshi. Hereby, the court announces three years rigorous punishment to Aaryan Rathod. The court is adjourned," said justice Verma and looked into my eyes. I could sense the satisfaction on his face. I folded my hand in respect of the judges and bowed my head to thank them. I was taken back to the jail to serve the sentenced period. My heart was pounding with happiness.

"Now I am going to meet Aarushi soon. We will get married and live life together forever. How best moments of my life were about to come."

Soon the judgement was shared with media. The news got spread like fire and everyone was shocked to hear the entire story. People who were eagerly waiting for me to be hanged were now raising slogans for my innocence. My parents got another life to live after listening to the judgment in the news channels. The news was also shared with Aarushi and listening to that she cried her heart out. The entire team of doctors and nurses attending Aarushi congratulated her and shared their happiness. Delhi was once again united, but this time to celebrate Aarushi's recovery and Himanshu's death. Though a few people thought what I did was wrong, but there were other class of citizens, mostly the young bloods, who thought what I did was the best way to punish a rapist. But, unlike a few days before, now everyone was happy to hear that I was not going to be hanged anymore.

Chapter 18
Three years

* * *

I lived a life with mixed emotions during the entire three years which I had to serve. I was happy that soon I will be out of the jail premises. But what hurt me the most was Aarushi didn't come to meet me in jail even for once. All she did for me was writing letters and send it across through Nikhil. I don't remember exactly that how many sleepless nights I had lived during these three years, crying and wondering why she was doing this to me. Through Nikhil and my parents, I came to know that she had cleared her IAS and had shifted to Lucknow. I sometimes felt, it would have been better if I would have got hanged that night instead of living a life of betrayal.

She had her dreams, but was I never her priority? Did she ever care to understand my feelings for her? Or she just considered me another lover of hers?

Letter1:

"Hi Aaryan,

I don't know what good I did in my last birth that God chose me to be with you. Why you felt I was that special girl on whom you would like to pour all your love. I still think do I really deserve you? You are such a kind and loving person that any girl would fall in love with you, but you chose me; a girl who did not even say, "I love you" to you. I am really blessed to have you in my life.

Aaryan, I am sorry. I know, if I had not come in your life, you would not have been in jail today. I am really sorry. I will never forgive myself for doing this to you. You aspired to become an Air Force officer and because of me, now you won't be able to fulfil your dream. Please forgive me.

I hope you would have heard the recording where I expressed my feelings for you. I could never acquire enough guts to say the same thing on your face. It was not that easy for me. But trust me, I always used to think about you while you were in office and I was in my hostel dumped in those thick books. I used to plan how I would ask you for another date. Remember, we went to temple. I just wanted to spend more time with you. You made me feel so special that sometimes I used to boast upon myself. You gave me more than what I would have even wished for.

On our first date, you could have kissed me, but you didn't. You don't know what that means to a girl. That day I realized the purity of your love. In love, it's not the body, but the soul that is involved; and you proved it. That night, when you were coming from Mysore, I planned to play my recording as soon as you enter the room. I had worn the same borrowed dress from Swati, which I wore for the club. I was looking pretty, and I am quite sure about it as Nikhil said he wished I had a twin sister. I had planned our first kiss. I was ready to get eaten by you.

But never in my worst dreams had I thought we would have to go through all these. I wish I could go back and change everything bad that happened to us. But, now nothing can be changed, so let's forget it.

I am recovering now and doctors say that I will be fine in another two months time. So don't worry about me. Please do take care of yourself and please don't share your stupid shayaris with other inmates :).

Just come out soon. The Java chip Frappuccino is still waiting for us :).

Lots of love and kisses,
Aarushi"

Letter 2:

"Hey Mr. Java, what's up?

I am really sorry, I could not visit you. I have been advised complete bed rest for next six months. I have got 18 stitches in my throat, which makes my life quite miserable. I can't speak much, but sometimes I take the pain to recite your stupid shayaris. Lying on the bed, I just prefer wandering around the imaginative world full of happiness and colours, with you by my side. It feels so amazing. I forget all my pains just by being with you even in my dreams.

Wish you would have been here to look after me and feed me with your hands. I am dying to see you. I now realise the true value of your irritating shayaris. Please write one more and handover to Nikhil when he visits you next time.

By the way you would be glad to know that, I have cleared the mains exam. After I saw the result I realized that if I would not have fallen for you, I would have been the topper.

But on a second thought, if you would not have fallen for me, I would have been just a topper and nothing else. Your unconditional love and care has anyway made me special. Because today I feel complete. I feel I achieved everything. And having you in my life makes me feel that, God gave me something, which I never dreamt of. You are the best thing that has ever happened to my life.

Please don't worry even a single moment for me. I am recovering fast and soon will come running to hug you. You take care of yourself. And please don't grow your beard to look like a serious prisoner. Beard doesn't suit you. And moreover, those little hair, will destroy my mood to kiss you. So keep yourself clean shaved. :)

Waiting for you,
Lots of love and kisses
Aarushi"

Letter-3

Dear Love,

Please don't get angry on me. I could not come to meet you even once and I really feel bad about it. But, I want you to understand my situation. After recovering from the surgeries, I was called for the interview. The interviewing panel were kind enough to offer me a grace period to recover. The interview went very good, and now your Aarushi is an IAS officer and now I have to move to Hyderabad for my training. Finally, I am able to realize my dreams.

I have got lots of pending stuffs to finish before I leave for Hyderabad. I am really sorry to sound selfish, but trust me I am helpless. I will wait for your release. And you have to promise me that you would be there on my passing out parade. I want you to put stars on my shoulders.

I met your parents too. They are really nice and I

feel you are blessed to have them as your parents. Your mom actually likes me and I have assured her that once I am back from my training, you and I will get married. I would love to be a part of this wonderful family. An orphan will get a family again, is it not amazing? I want to get married to you and have kids. I want to be kissed by you every moment. I want you to love me forever. Please never hate me.

Yours
Aarushi.

This was the last letter I received from Aarushi. Thereafter, she didn't find any time for me. It was tough for me to convince myself that she was not doing it intentionally. *My Aarushi can never betray me,* was the only statement I used to give myself to pacify my heart.

The mere thought of her betrayal used to bring rallies of tears in my eyes. Why it was always about her dreams that she cared? Why did she save me from getting hanged if this is what she had to do to me later? There were millions of questions in my heart, but there was no one to answer them.

"Yeh waqt bhi na jaane kaun si gunaho ki saza de raha hai mujhko

Thak gaya hu ab is dil ko manate, jo har pal keh raha hai bewafaa tujhko."

Chapter 19
And I met Aarushi

❄ ❄ ❄

Time came when I was going to start my new life after spending three years in prison. I had a fear in my heart. Though, I was confident that Aarushi won't betray me, but somewhere because she didn't visit me anytime during those three years, except sending letters through Nikhil, I was little worried about what if she married someone else. After all she was now an IAS officer and definitely she would have got many proposals from best of the guys in the world. I was getting restless just by the thought of spending the rest of my life without Aarushi.

I was handed all my stuff packed in a carton that were kept by the jail authorities during my trial.

"Thank you Sir," I said signing the last formality letter and handing it to Ali sir.

"Aaryan, now as you are free, I want you to understand this. Please grab the chair if you can afford a little more time with me," said Ali Sir. I politely sat on the chair he offered to me.

"The crime you committed was not your fault. Any human being would have done that if they would have been at your place. But, as Mahatma Gandhi said, "An eye for an eye will leave the world blind," we should not take law in our hands. I know it is easy to say than doing, but I really feel sorry when someone educated like you end up behind the bars because of these unthoughtful steps," said Ali Sir with concern on his face.

I understood what he meant. I remained silent as I could not have agreed anymore.

"I, too, understand that there are lots of flaws in our judicial system, but all that needs to be questioned, discussed and fixed. That does not mean that till it is not fixed, we take law in our hands. Boys like Himanshu does not deserve to live alive, but unfortunately our judicial system is slow and men like him escape. Hundreds of rape cases are registered every day in our country, and what do you think is the reason behind it?"asked Ali sir raising his voice in frustration. I knew, he didn't want me to answer, but to listen.

"The reason is that no one is afraid of law. Criminals know that if they have power and money, they can easily escape punishment and can bypass court trial. And sadly many rape cases don't get registered because the victim knows about our judicial system which would keep them waiting for years for the judgement to arrive. I feel sorry for all those victims. I carry this handcuff, but you know what, it is me whose hand is cuffed by so called law," said Ali sir throwing the handcuffs on the floor.

I then stood to offer him a glass of water and requested him to calm down. His eyes were moist, but he was strong enough to hold his tears.

"Ali Sir, today I am satisfied that we do have people

like you serving our country. You are not like those who run their family selling their dignity. I am sure our country will change. People will grow mature to differentiate between good and bad. We won't wait for the candle march, but we will lit the spark inside us to ask for stringent law against rapists, so that next time no one should even remotely think to destroy a girl's life," I expressed my anger.

Ali Sir nodded his head and prayed to the almighty for making our country a safest place to live in. He bid me final adieu and walked me to the exit.

"There is a great life waiting for you out there," said Ali sir. The guards at the door opened the exit gate for me to step into my new life.

After having a good discussion with Ali sir, I was feeling positive about myself. I was excited to start everything again. And moreover, I was happy that now I need not to work hard to impress Aarushi as she had already expressed her feelings. I was clean shaved as asked by Aarushi in one of her letters, hoping that she would plant a soft and passionate kiss over my cheeks. It was a long time we saw each other.

"God please stop me from crying and keep me as cool as you can when I see Aarushi," I made a silent prayer.

"Here comes our hero," shouted Nikhil after he saw me coming out of the exit gate. I was happy to see my parents and Nikhil, who came to receive me. I looked around for Aarushi, but she was not there. She had promised me in her last letter that she would come to receive me, but she didn't.

It hurts a lot when someone whom you love so much doesn't care about your feelings.

"Welcome back hero," said Nikhil hugging me. I broke into tears. It had been three years that the two best friends had hugged each other.

I bowed down to touch my parents' feet and take their blessings. They too had tears in their eyes, but this time it was coming out of happiness to see me free.

"Thank you so much. You never gave up on me," I said folding my hands to offer them my gratitude. They hugged me and cried their heart out.

"You should be thankful to Aarushi, who gave her statement or else we could not have seen this day," said Ma wiping her tears with her sari's veil.

"Yes, but where is she? She promised that she would come here to receive me," I asked.

My mom looked at Nikhil accepting him to answer. Nikhil looked quite tensed to hear that. He stepped forward and said, "We are going to meet Aarushi. Come take a seat," opening the rear door of the cab. I was excited to hear that. Finally I was going to meet Aarushi.

"Is this all planned by her?" I asked sitting at the rear with my parents. I was behaving like a kid, smiling for no sense.

"Yes, it was her plan," answered Nikhil.

"Mom, dad, would you mind if I get married to her today?" I asked looking at my parents. They looked at each other for an answer and then nodded their head to accept. I hugged my mom as she was the one who was sitting closer to me. "Thank you so much. I love you," I said to my mom.

"Leave all this. Were you not eating all these days? Look at you. You look like a stick," said mom inspecting me from top to bottom.

I agreed as I had lost a few kilos, but I was not at all thin like a stick. This is the problem with all moms on the planet. For them, no matter how fat you are, they will always look at you as the thinnest creature on the Earth, My mom was no different.

"In jail they don't put butter over chapatti, but over their baton. And unfortunately, having those oily batons, doesn't add to weight. I had a lot of those," I said smiling to which my mom started crying.

"Where are we going? I have never been on this route before," I asked when the driver took turn towards the countryside. Nikhil gestured driver to keep driving and not to talk. I pinched Nikhil from behind and said, "*Sale, kuch surprise plan kiya hai kya* (You rascal have you planned some surprise or what?)" to which Nikhil nodded his head and asked me to sit quietly.

"Mom, I know that your soon to be daughter-in-law has made you her co-conspirator. Please tell me what the surprise is. If by any chance you guys are planning my engagement ceremony then please tell me, I need to dress well. I don't want to regret later when I see my pictures," I said pleading to my mom. She placed my head over her shoulder and asked me to close my eyes until we arrive at the surprise spot.

Leaned over my mom's shoulder with my eyes shut, I relived all those beautiful moments I spent with Aarushi. Teasing her with my shayaris, making her life miserable, and then our first date, which was screwed because of my stupidity. The night when Aarushi shared her dark past with me and the temple visit, every single moment made a comeback like a wonderful memory. I was excited and was dying to meet Aarushi.

"What would I say to her? Will it be okay if I kiss her in front of mom and dad? Will she like it? or Should I wait until marriage?," all these questions encircled my brain.

After another fifteen minutes of drive the car stopped.

"Don't open your eyes" said Nikhil. My mom too closed my eyes with her palm. I could hear some wedding band sound coming from a distant.

"God, they have planned my wedding," I thought and laughed madly. Nikhil covered my eyes with a piece of cloth and held my hand while we walked through some forest. The reason why I guessed it was a forest as I could feel stepping over bushes and grasses. The band sound was getting louder as we were approaching towards the surprise spot.

"Bhai, don't do this to me. Please remove this band from my eyes. I can easily hear the band sound. You guys are not the best surprise planners," I said struggling to peek outside from the covered eyes. Nikhil didn't say anything and simple kept taking me along with him. Neither my mom nor my dad had a mercy on me. They too ignored my pleading.

After approximately ten minutes of walk Nikhil finally stopped.

"What, are you done? Come on let's walk another few miles," I taunted.

"Aaryan, kneel down," said Nikhil.

"What? Now I know what you guys have planned. Aarushi, I know you are there, so stop bluffing anymore. Please at least you show some mercy on me," I pleaded to Aarushi, but got no reply.

"Fine," I said kneeling down, "At least give me the engagement ring," I asked.

Nikhil uncovered my eyes. My heart started pounding faster than ever. I was going to look at my love, my life after three years. I took a deep breath and said, "Aarushi, I won't open my eyes until you hug me. Please don't feel shy because of my parents being here. They won't mind," I said spreading my hands wide to embrace Aarushi.

I could not sense any movement from Aarushi, so I requested her again to hug me. With my eyes still closed, I started moving my hands in the air to catch Aarushi, but then my hand hit over a stone. I opened my eyes out of pain.

"In loving memory of Aarushi Rathod," I read the

name embarked over a grave. I froze. I could not believe that she was no more. My Aarushi was buried inside the grave. I was losing my breath. Feeling restless, I wanted to dig that grave and hug her. I started hitting her grave and pleaded Aarushi to come out.

"Aarushi, please for god sake come out. You cannot leave me alone like this. See, I have shaved my beard too for you. I promise I will never ever trouble you. Please Aarushi, please come out I can't live without you. I have to see you. My eyes are dying to see you please. I love you yaar, why are you not listening to me. I waited three long years to see you and now you left me alone. Please, please come out," I cried over her grave. Hugged her grave tightly to feel her in my arms,but she didn't come out.

My parents could not see me in that condition, but they restricted themselves from stopping me to cry. Nikhil, took hold of me and pulled me away from the grave. He handed me a steel box which was kept beside the grave. With teary eyes, I opened the box. It had all the letters that I used to write for Aarushi while I was there in the jail. It also had that rose, which I gifted her once, her favourite nose ring, few bangles, and a closed envelope.

"My last letter to the love of my life" was written on the envelope. I opened to read her last letter to me.

"Hello Mr. Java,

I am 100 per cent sure; you know that I am no more. That bastard killed me, but he could not kill our love story and trust me, no one can.

You know I still feel the pain I went through. I still have the scars on my face. That night horrifies me. I was recording my feelings for you in my cell phone and then the doorbell rang Anticipating you, I ran to give a quick makeover to myself as I wanted to look as beautiful as you used to describe me in your shayaris, but when I opened the door, Himanshu hit my stomach with his leg so hard that I could not gather enough strength to stand back. Then they did what they came for. I was raped brutally. When I yelled for help, Himanshu slit my throat. I was bleeding and nearing to death. At that moment, the only regret that I had was, I could not see you. I wished you would have been there with me that time. I would have preferred dying in your arms than dying on the hospital bed. It's so tough for a girl to live a secured life in our country. My death is going to make no difference either. So let's forget it.

I know, you must have been hurt to the core of your heart as I didn't visit you even once while you were in jail. Please forgive me. Also forgive Nikhil as I asked him not to share this with you. I preferred you to hate me than to spend your three years in a grief of losing me forever.

Enough of serious talks. Nikhil told me that you were writing a story to let India know what happened to us. Hats off to engineers! Really, you guys can be productive even in jail. Engineers don't leave a single opportunity to show off :) Once you finish that book, please sign it and keep it on my grave. I would like to read our love story.

Now as you are here; let me assure you, I have gone nowhere, I am watching you reading my last letter. I am not as good as you in playing with words to express feelings, but this is the best a dying girl can write.

Things can't be changed now, so stop crying. Tears don't suit you and "Pushpa, I hate tears" :)

You gave me a life I dreamt of. I never thought I would be loved by someone so madly and honestly. You made me the princess of your heart. I kept hurting you, but you never gave up. What else an orphan could have wished for! Every second spent with you was a life for me. If you would not have come in to my life, I would have never realised what love means.

Feelings for you started from the day we met at the temple. And I loved it when you covered my head with a dupatta. I wanted to give you a tight hug, but that would have encouraged you to do more of stupidity so I killed my desires. I never thought I would die so soon. Had I known it before, trust me I would not have stopped myself from expressing my feelings for you. But anyway, I will always be with you. You just need to feel my presence.

Aaryan, it's time you accept the hard truth. It's time you look forward to your life. Don't spoil your life worrying about the past. I had the best time of my life and that was enough for me. So don't keep any regrets in your heart. I was destined for this, but you are not. You need to go and chase your dreams. I want to see you in Air Force uniform. And please, once you become an officer, do bring a Ray Ban glasses for me too. You can keep it over my grave. I will show off here to the Angels.

I want you to get married and live a life that you always wanted to live. Marry a girl of your choice. Love does happen twice. Never ever think how I would feel to see you in someone else's life. I will be more than happy to see that happening. I will be satisfied that someone is there with you to take care of you and give you all the love which I could not. But promise me, you will never forget me. Promise me that once in a day you will think of me. Pardon me if I am asking for more, but trust me, I am a wandering soul, just to be with you.

Before you leave, please write a shayari for me. I have been waiting so long to listen to one. It should better be good or else I will haunt you at night :)

Keep smiling and never cry; this dead girl is so helpless that she cannot even wipe your tears.

Lots of love and kisses

Yours and only yours... Aarushi"

My tears dried. I was looking all around for Aarushi. I wished to die and get buried beside her. How can I live the rest of my life without her? Why did she leave me alone, knowing that she was the only reason I have been living for? How can she ask me to get married to someone else? There were other hundreds of questions which I knew would never be answered.

I asked Nikhil as how I was kept unknown about Aarushi's death for three years. This news was making rounds in media and social network then how come it never came to me. Nikhil and my parents had requested Ali sir not to share this news with me. Ali sir assured that he would never share this with me. Aarushi had died the next day after she gave her statement to the police. I don't know if what they did was right or not, but I will live a life with a regret that I was not there with Aarushi during her last breath.

As asked by Aarushi, I wrote a shayari and kept it in the box before leaving.

"Tujhe bhula sakhu, woh bahana khojta hu
Apne dil ko behla saku, woh fasana khojta hu
Jis Bhagwan ki log khaate hai kasme, woh Bhagwan khojta hu
Meri ruuh jo tere sath chali gayi, Aaj ussi ruuh ko khojta hu"